Asylum

Sarah Hans

RAW DOG SCREAMING PRESS

Published by Raw Dog Screaming Press
Bowie, MD
First Edition

Cover art copyright 2023 by Lynne Hansen
LynneHansenArt.com
Book Design by Jennifer Barnes
"Simply, a Note" by Vaughn A. Jackson

Printed in the United States of America

ISBN: 978-1-947879-68-3

Library of Congress Control Number:
2024930064
RawDogScreaming.com

Asylum

Sarah Hans

Also by Sarah Hans

Goodnight Halloween

Entomophobia

Dead Girls Don't Love

An Ideal Vessel

to Anton Cancre, my Wonder Twin

Simply, a Note

The human mind is a strange and tedious thing. Memory—fickle and flighty, yet vicious and ironclad—locks you into a mold, an illusory pattern that guides your lives. You act, and you remember, over and over, but you don't always learn, do you? There is comfort in patterns, in structure, and order even when they shift from guidelines to bars on a cage around your lives. Freedom brings with it fear of the unknown, of slipping through the gaps in the webs you weave. It's funny I say "*you*" when those who work here are strung along their own pattern—constantly collecting and compiling *Selected Papers from the Consortium for the Study of Anomalous Phenomena.* Buried deep in the dust-laden basement of the university's library, they toil like parched men, or women, scouring the dankest corners for just one drop of water. Page after page, they read beneath the pale yellow glow of ancient bulbs until their eyes bulge and burn with each passing word. Hours of discomfort, but at the end they always walk away with *something*. This time, Sarah Hans' *Asylum.*

Patterns grip at the heart of each character in Asylum—cycles of violence, addiction, and trauma—tearing them apart from the inside like the claws of a…well, perhaps it's best if you discover *that* on your own.

Despite her in-depth analysis of patterns and their effects, Hans herself is quite the wildcard: author, editor, teacher. From Steampunk to *Selected Papers*, and with so many dead girls in between. Her work has been raised up by Dragon's Roost Press and that eldritch beast, *io9*. And yet, even here we see a pattern—one of success and publication repeating once more with this very manuscript. How novel. But, I digress...

While the previous manuscript, *12 Hours* I believe it was, "delved into the human psyche utilizing minutia often taken for granted,", *Asylum* expands this microcosm into a macrocosm of several meth addicts, each haunted by their own traumas, but bound together by their greatest vice—an odd, twisted sort of family. There's a feral thread running through this group of misfits well before all the cats show up. Contention brought to a head by withdrawal, isolation, misplaced trust, and plays for redemption.

Once you've woven a web around yourself, trying to escape will leave you tangled. Ashleigh, the protagonist, learns this all too well as her group spirals out of control from within, and without. It's not just meth addicts and cats locked behind the abandoned cement walls of the titular Asylum. We follow her throughout its empty halls and beneath strange moonlights while she tries to escape her own pattern of bad decisions, only to find herself tangled in a reality she never could have expected. One she very well may carry with her the rest of her life. Perhaps her life is a pattern on new cages... perhaps that's all any of your lives are. Or perhaps not.

After all, I'm not The Professor, how should I know?

Did you think I was? Again, trying to fall into patterns. Humans! No, I merely...linger in the corners where the shadows have settled. I've been disturbed by recent activities—a pattern I'm sure will continue for some time.

Regardless, listening to the scholars, they seemed quite pleased with what they found. They were crying, though that may have been the dust raining down from above. One claimed that "Hans shows that destructive cycles can be broken, but doesn't sugar coat the lasting impact that they have on those caught in them.". He said more, but as before I don't wish to spoil the narrative. Another of the scholars simply said, "Be careful who you trust."

Wise words. For a human.

I'm sure, given the aura of those well-dusted men and women, that the release of this manuscript will be met with intrigue and excitement. As with the last, and the one before that…a pattern, once more. May the webs you weave support, but never tangle, and the threads you follow lead you ever forward.

Repeatedly Yours,
The Weaver

Chapter 1

Ashleigh had become accustomed to living in chaos. Still, when Connor came home and dropped a gun on the coffee table, she felt something snap inside her. He was sweaty and wild-eyed and paced the room like a caged animal. She barely heard him rambling about how they had to leave, they had to find somewhere to go, and it had to be right away, because her mind could only think about how this must be what rock-bottom felt like. She didn't want to do this anymore.

Dean came into the room with a duffel bag. "Calm down and pack your shit, man."

Connor whirled and shot Dean a death-glare. Dean held up his hands placatingly, averting his eyes from Connor's face. Connor's hands fisted at his sides and there was a tense moment where everyone froze, prepared for the usual violence. Then, abruptly, he stomped out of the room.

"What the hell happened?" Ashleigh asked, sitting up from the couch where she'd been languishing all day, dozing and watching TikToks on her phone.

Dean shook his head and looked at the floor. Sweat had soaked through the t-shirt that clung to his lean frame. His hands shook.

"Connor got a gun in trade and thought it would be a good idea to hold up the corner store."

Ashleigh gaped at him, panic zinging her nerves to full alertness. "The corner store…around the corner from *here*? Why didn't you stop him? What the fuck were you thinking? And then you came back here?!"

"We thought we could pull it off. But a cop walked in and we had to run. We're fine, by the way. All the shots went wide."

Connor did stupid shit when he was high, but this was by far the dumbest thing he'd ever done. Ashleigh's ears filled with a weird buzzing sound, the sound of mounting panic. This squat was the best one they'd found in months. They hadn't even been caught yet, so no eviction proceedings were processing. They could have potentially lived here for months, through the winter even. But Connor and Dean had to go fucking it up.

Ashleigh bit her tongue when Connor came back into the room. She wanted to scream at him, but she knew what the result would be, especially when he was high as balls and adrenaline was ripping through his bloodstream. Her stomach cramped with the willpower required to resist the rage that made her feel like her blood was on fire.

Connor tossed a bulging laptop bag on the coffee table, knocking beer cans and an ashtray to the floor. "Why aren't you packed? We need to get out of here."

Ashleigh opened her mouth to respond, but a police siren wailed down the street. Connor threw himself to the floor and Dean followed a second later. Ashleigh stood over them, shaking her head and crossing her arms across her chest. The police car raced past the house, the siren fading into the afternoon. "You are such morons," she told them, kicking a beer can out of her way as she stormed into the bedroom.

Connor followed her. "That was a bitchy thing to say."

"You robbed the corner store, the one two blocks away! The cops will be here any minute." As she spoke, Ashleigh pulled clothes from the dilapidated dresser they'd rescued from the alley a few blocks away when some renters were evicted. She shoved the clothes into a trash bag, the same one she'd dragged here the last time they'd moved. "I'm done, Connor. This is too much."

"Baby, baby, you can't say that." His strong hands closed on her upper arms and he turned her toward him.

She wouldn't meet his eyes. "You're gonna get arrested and you'll go to prison and I'll be all alone. I might as well go back to my dad now."

Connor pulled her close, pressing her against his lean chest, surrounding her with his masculine scent. "No, baby, no. It's gonna blow over. We just need a place to lay low for a while. We can go to Eliot's place. Nobody knows us over there."

Ashleigh jerked away from him. "Eliot? That fucking gross-ass rapist? I'm not staying in a house with him." She shoved the last of her belongings into the bag. "Besides, I wanna get clean. Can't do that at Eliot's place."

"You want to get clean?" Connor said it like the idea was a surprise to him, like she hadn't been talking about it for weeks.

"I don't want this life anymore. You can have it." She brushed past him to the door.

Connor's long fingers closed around her arm and dragged her back to him. "You don't want to make another baby with me anymore?" He sounded so hurt, it made her lungs clench. His fingers brushed her neck and sent a shiver across her skin.

Ashleigh tightened her grip on the trash bag and grit her teeth. "I'm not gonna have a baby in this body. Maybe ever. I'm not even sure I want one. Right now I just want to focus on getting clean." Maybe then, the answers would be clearer.

Connor wrapped his long arms around her, pressing his lips against her temple. "Then I guess we should go somewhere we can get clean."

Dean appeared in the hall. "Are you two coming?"

Ashleigh looked up at Connor over her shoulder. "You mean it?"

He smiled that smile of his, that charming smile that made her melt, that smile that was somehow sad and hopeful at the same time. His eyes met hers, so intense, so intimate. She felt seen when he looked at her like that, like she was the only person in the world. He traced the shape of her jaw with his fingers. "Of course. Maybe we can get a motel room or something."

"We don't have any money," Dean said loudly.

"Kayla might," Connor replied.

Dean sighed. "We shouldn't get Kayla involved."

"You would just leave without her?" Ashleigh asked.

"I think it would be best if she didn't get involved in all this, yeah," Dean confirmed.

Connor took the trash bag from Ashleigh and hefted it over his shoulder. "She's the one with a car and money, dumbass. We need her."

Dean scratched at the back of his neck and stared at the floor. "She's so young. She's only been using for a few weeks. She can still get out, Connor."

Connor shoved past Dean into the living room. "You're the one who gave her that first taste, man. Besides, she loves you. She's not just going to let you go."

"That's why we don't tell her."

Ashleigh studied Dean's face in the dim hall lighting. "You would leave without telling her? Without saying anything? You'd just...ghost her?"

Dean slapped the wall. "Goddammit, Ashleigh, it's the best thing for her. I'm no good. None of us are."

From the living room there came the sound of Connor having a one-sided conversation. Ashleigh and Dean rushed into the room. Connor had Ashleigh's phone pressed to his ear. "Yeah, don't worry about the job. You can get another one. We need to get out of here now. It's an—"

Dean snatched the phone from him, tossing it across the room. Kayla's voice issued from it, high and panicked. The two men grappled while Ashleigh found the device under the threadbare recliner.

"Just come home," she instructed Kayla, and then hung up.

"Goddammit, Ashleigh!" Dean shouted. He raised his fist and Ashleigh fell to her knees automatically.

Connor, five inches taller and stronger in every way, grabbed Dean's shoulder and tossed him to the floor effortlessly. "Don't touch her."

Ashleigh scrambled to her feet. "It's okay, Connor. I'm okay."

"It's not okay." Connor was fuming again, getting himself worked up. "Apologize to Ashleigh," he commanded Dean.

Dean picked himself up off the floor, straightened his t-shirt, and mumbled, "Sorry, Ashleigh."

Connor grabbed him by the front of his shirt, pulling Dean so close their noses nearly touched. "Don't you ever fucking touch my girl, you understand? You ever do that again and you'll be the armless wonder."

"Yeah, man," Dean croaked. "I get it."

That was the one good thing about Dean: he usually backed down from Connor before any real violence happened. He knew his place.

Ashleigh went to the kitchen and started pulling whatever food she could find from the cabinets.

Connor followed her. "What're you doing?"

"We'll need food, wherever we're going. You guys get toilet paper, soap, whatever else we have." Kayla had done a grocery run that week so they were, luckily, fully stocked. Ashleigh found a cardboard box under the heap of trash in the corner of the kitchen and started tossing boxes of snack cakes and packages of ramen noodles into it. She threw in a pot she'd stolen from a neighbor when they'd left their back door unlocked, and the bowls and utensils she'd stolen from the restaurant where she held a waitressing job a few months ago.

Connor turned but then hesitated in the doorway. "You have a plan, don't you? Where do you think we're going?"

Ashleigh drew in a breath for courage. "The asylum."

Connor made an incredulous sound, like a bark. "I already told you no, no way. That place is creepy. It's too far from civilization and there's no electricity, no water—"

She turned to face him, planting her feet firmly and placing her hands on her hips. "And it's the last place anyone would look for us. For *you*. You've made it so we don't have a choice. Besides, it's not like we have electricity or water here, either."

Connor licked his lips and swayed, his posture tense, as if he wanted to argue. But then he nodded, wagging a finger at her, and his body relaxed. "That's brilliant. You're brilliant, babe."

He went out of the kitchen and Dean took his place. "The asylum?"

Ashleigh folded her arms over her chest. She was a few inches shorter than he was, and he had probably forty pounds on her, but she wasn't intimidated, not by Dean. She raised her chin, as she had many times before, and stared him down with unflinching eye contact. "Yeah. The asylum."

Dean's nostrils flared and he sucked his teeth, but after a few seconds of staring at the floor, he backed down.

She gestured to the box. "Finish packing this. I'm going to find what else we can bring with us."

Chapter 2

Kayla didn't want to drive them to the asylum. She didn't even
want to leave the house. It took Dean nearly an hour to convince
her the asylum on the mountain was their best option. Ashleigh,
meanwhile, kept Connor calm in the back bedroom. He wanted to
steal Kayla's keys and go without her and while Ashleigh found
that tempting, Kayla was the most useful person in their fucked up
little family right now. Besides, she'd definitely report the stolen
car to the cops and that would make them even more vulnerable
than they were now.

While Kayla sniffled in the driver's seat, Ashleigh placed the
packed bags and boxes in the trunk and climbed into the passenger
seat. When everything was ready, Connor and Dean walked
hurriedly from the house and slid into the backseat. Dean, barely
more substantial than an aluminum folding chair, sat on the floor.
Connor laid down on the seat with his legs tucked up. They looked
ridiculous, like some kind of abstract performance art piece, and
Ashleigh swallowed a grim laugh.

"Do you know how to get there?" Kayla asked, looking at
Ashleigh with watery eyes.

Ashleigh nodded and gave directions. She'd figured it out months ago, the first time she'd suggested the asylum as a good home base. Excitement and dread warred inside her. They were finally going to get clean; she would finally get to have the life she dreamed of with Connor. No more selling drugs, no more living in abandoned houses until they were caught and evicted. No more shitting in buckets and burying it in the yard, stealing electricity from neighbors, drinking rainwater, or reading tattered paperbacks by flashlight at night.

Things had been better when Ashleigh had been working. After a series of jobs that lasted no more than a few weeks, she'd gotten a job at the UDF a few blocks away. She'd liked that job. It was easy, and her boss was a customer of Connor's, so she didn't get in trouble if she was late for a shift. They had smoked all her income, of course, but that was okay, too. Wasn't that what money was for? She had squirreled some away every paycheck in the hopes of eventually having first month's rent for a real place of their own, where they could have electricity, heat, air conditioning, running water—all the luxuries she'd had once, before crystal became more important than any of those things.

But then she got pregnant. She didn't know right away, of course. She was three months in before she realized she hadn't had a period in a long time. She'd thought she was too skinny to have a baby. Crystal made it hard to keep on weight, and when she was really thin, Ashleigh just didn't bleed. It was like her body was saying she was too weak and her insides too toxic to produce life.

Two pregnancy tests had confirmed it, though. Ashleigh had been terrified. She'd never wanted kids. She was happy with Connor's attention all to herself, and she didn't know how to be a good mother, anyway. Her own mother hadn't exactly been a shining example, though Ashleigh did admit she'd kept the lights on and the plumbing working in their little house, even as she went missing for days at a time on booze-fueled benders.

Ashleigh had gotten high to deal with the stress of the pregnancy. She knew it might endanger the fetus, but at the time she didn't care. She'd been smoking the whole three months she was unaware of the pregnancy, so, what did one more time matter? If she had the baby it would be fucked up either way.

The miscarriage hadn't hurt. She'd woken up with blood soaked into the mattress and Connor panicking over her, thinking she was bleeding to death. Ashleigh hadn't wanted the baby, but she still cried and cried when she woke up after surgery and learned it was gone. So maybe she did want it. She still wasn't sure.

Thinking about it made tears prick at her eyes, so she shoved the painful feeling in her stomach down, down, until she couldn't feel it anymore. Until she was just a head with no connection to her body, like a balloon. She could just drift away into a book or, if her dad had paid her cell phone bill, into social media, or shows on streaming services. She didn't know why her dad kept paying the cell phone bill, but she suspected it was so that he and her stepmom could have some small evidence she was alive when she made a post on Instagram or watched a movie on their Netflix. That was a trade Ashleigh was willing to make, as long as she didn't have to talk to them, or see them. They wanted her to come home. They wanted her to give up Connor, and she just couldn't do that. She'd tried, twice, in fact, and both times she'd gone back to him. Something about him was just irresistible to her, like he was a negative magnet and she was a positive one and they couldn't stop touching each other. She could feel his pull from miles away, maybe across entire galaxies. Their relationship felt like destiny.

Kayla followed the directions and turned onto a residential street. Eventually the houses spaced themselves further and further apart as the car wound its way up the mountainside. The sidewalks disappeared and the road became uneven and pitted. Then it was just gravel and the little car struggled with the steep incline. And then the road just seemed to end, and they could go no further in the car. Tall grass, massive shrubs, and skinny saplings blocked the way, nature reclaiming what mankind had once built. In the distance, the blocky gray asylum was sharp like a blade against the soft blue sky.

"This is it," Ashleigh said, unbuckling her seatbelt when Kayla applied the brakes.

"What do you mean?" Kayla asked. She peered out the windshield as if the asylum had a valet who would come out from behind a tree and ask for her keys.

"We have to go on foot from here. The road was allowed to grow over years ago."

"We have to *walk?*"

"Why do you think I told you to wear your sneakers?" Ashleigh climbed out of the car and went to the trunk. "It's not far. Come and get your shit."

Kayla followed her. "That looks really steep."

Connor and Dean unfolded themselves from the backseat and stretched, groaning. "She said it's not far," Connor told Kayla. "It's just a little climb, right, babe?"

Ashleigh pulled a box from the trunk and tossed her trash bag and a few bottles of water into it. "I never said it would be easy." She grabbed a bungee cord from the trunk and tied it around the hand-hold on the side of the box. Then she turned and headed for the overgrown path, pulling the box behind her like a trashy sled.

Chapter 3

The others were taller than Ashleigh, so it wasn't long before they caught up to her, though they were all burdened. Ashleigh suspected some things had been left behind with the car, but she supposed they could always return for them later. As long as they had food and water they would be okay—the rest, they could figure out.

The forest was peaceful and quiet. An occasional breeze ruffled the leaves of the large trees on either side of the remnants of the road, and birds chirped piercing songs. The air smelled cleaner than anything Ashleigh could remember smelling ever in her life. She smiled, delighted that she would have access to this peace just outside the doorstep of their new home. This was a really good idea. Connor was right, she was brilliant.

The overgrown road got steep though. Ashleigh's calves started to burn. She propped the box against a sapling. "I've got to pee," she told the others, and walked into the trees. They had all seen her naked before, so she wasn't sure why she wanted privacy. It just didn't seem right to squat in the middle of the grass with the sun shining down on her and birds wheeling overhead.

She found a ditch not far from the road and dropped her shorts to her knees. She gripped a tree trunk and leaned back a little as a torrent of urine poured from her body. Peeing downhill was a skill her mother had taught her. Ashleigh wondered if she would someday teach her own daughter how to piss in the woods without getting it on her shoes. The thought gave her a surge of emotion behind her breastbone, though she couldn't quite identify what the emotion was.

A few crunching steps and Connor appeared a few feet from her. He unzipped his jeans and his urine joined hers in the ditch. His piss smelled strong and Ashleigh wrinkled her nose. She made a mental note to make him drink more water.

She remained in a crouch for a few more seconds to drip-dry. Then she stood and pulled up her shorts. She groaned with pain as the movement made her leg muscles scream.

The sound of the rattlesnake was like someone shaking a bottle full of very tiny pills. Ashleigh froze, some primal instinct telling her not to move. She looked slowly down at the ground. Beside her right foot a brown timber rattler was nearly invisible in the undergrowth. Its beady eyes were fixed on her leg and its rattle vibrated furiously while it tasted the air with a forked tongue.

"Babe? You okay?" Connor asked, taking a step toward her.

"Stop!" Ashleigh commanded. "Rattlesnake."

Connor froze. "Oh, fuck. There's rattlesnakes up here?" He looked furtively in the undergrowth until he spotted the snake. "Aw, it's just a little fucker. Kind of cute."

"The little ones have the worst bite," Ashleigh said. Her voice was a high, tremulous whisper. Her heart pounded and fear made her vision ragged at the edges, but she kept her eyes on the snake. What was she going to do? If she moved, it might strike. Her best bet for survival was to stand completely still until the snake calmed down and moved away—

Suddenly, without any warning, Connor used a long stick to knock the rattlesnake away, issuing a little shout of triumph as the legless body twisted through the air. Ashleigh ran to the road of grass like the devil was on her heels. She plunged through the trees and into the sunlight, where the instant warmth and brightness was like a whole different world. A safer world.

"What happened?" Kayla asked as Dean simultaneously said, "You okay, Ash?"

Ashleigh nodded, so out of breath she couldn't speak. She found a clear piece of earth and knelt there, putting her hands on the dirt to ground herself.

Connor exploded from the trees whooping and whipping the stick around his head like he'd just defeated the Balrog and not a snake barely a foot long. "Ash found a rattler," he announced. "But it's okay, I took care of it." He puffed out his chest and propped the stick against his shoulder like a knight with his sword.

"Seriously?" Kayla squeaked. "There are *snakes* up here?"

Ashleigh shrugged. Kayla's voice sounded far away and thin. "I guess."

Dean approached her and placed one hand on her shoulder. "Are you sure you didn't get bit?"

Ashleigh nodded. "I'm sure."

"I saved her life," Connor announced proudly. "And maybe some others, too. I don't think that snake's gonna be bothering anyone else anytime soon."

"You're very brave," Kayla said flatly, her eyes never leaving Ashleigh's doubled-over form.

"It's okay now. You're safe." Dean rubbed circles on her back. "Try to just breathe." He offered her a water bottle.

Ashleigh inhaled and exhaled, her galloping heartbeat slowing. She drank a few swallows of water. When she had regained control of herself, she nodded at Dean and he helped her stand. "Let's keep going."

"Well I was gonna suggest that cutting through the woods might get us there sooner," Dean said, grimacing up at the asylum. They were close enough now to see the sun reflected in the huge windows overlooking Perrysville, like many golden, glowing eyes.

"No way." Kayla answered before Ashleigh could.

They lifted their burdens and resumed their long trudge. They moved in silence. Connor walked at the front, now, sweeping the grass with his stick like a blind man looking for obstacles. The others followed, hoping the path he cut would be free of snakes and other biting creatures. Ashleigh found herself falling into a sort of trance, her mind numb, drifting like a cloud in a strong breeze. If she let her consciousness come back into her body there was too much pain and fear, so instead she let it float away. She'd become very good at floating away from reality, but it was easier with crystal. She longed for it, for how easy and content it made her feel. Meth made all the bad thoughts go away.

She shook her head in an attempt to clear the craving. She needed to be stronger than this! They weren't even 24 hours from their last smoke. The cravings and withdrawal symptoms were going to get a lot worse.

They weren't far from the asylum when a scream sliced through the quiet. Ashleigh turned to see Kayla staring at something on the ground. Her knees buckled and her arms releasing the bags she'd been carrying. Connor and Dean rushed to her side and looked at whatever Kayla had found.

"Oh, fuck. Ashleigh." Connor gestured for her to come toward them, never taking his eyes off whatever it was that had them so freaked out.

Ashleigh propped her box against a rock jutting from the grass and let go of the bungee cord. She walked over to her friends, took a deep breath, and turned to face whatever it was.

A mangled carcass, blood and guts and fur in a nonsensical jumble, intestines already turned gray with rot, was lying in the grass. It was twisted and mauled so badly Ashleigh couldn't identify it right away, but as her mind made sense of the black and bloody mess, she realized it was a coyote, with its insides on the outside, intestines still glistening. Ashleigh had gone hunting with her dad a lot as a kid, and she'd seen many dead animals killed in various ways. She'd seen animals killed by other animals before, and this didn't look like that. While the carcass appeared to have died a violent death courtesy of a large predator, the tears in the coyote's skin were long and clean, as if they'd been made by a sharp hunting knife. And it looked like all the major parts were still there—none of the dead coyote had been eaten.

Ashleigh blinked at it for a few seconds, considering how much her friends needed to know, and then shrugged. "It's a coyote."

"Well, duh," Connor said. "But what the hell happened to it?"

"Probably a bear." The smell of decay hit her then and she swallowed against her gag reflex.

Dean shook his head. "There aren't any bears around here."

"It's gotta be Perry," Kayla said in a soft whisper, as if she were afraid to speak it into being.

"You're not serious," Connor said. "There is no Perry the Panther. That's just a dumb story."

Perry the Panther was a Perrysville legend that seemed to resurrect itself every few years as a new batch of teenagers found their way to the woods outside town to smoke and fuck. They'd hear some strange noises or find some animal remains and name Perry as the culprit so they could sprint back to civilization, back to their nice safe beds in their nice warm houses. It was a little thrill of fear on a chill autumn night, that was all. Perry wasn't real.

"My uncle told me that story is true," Dean said.

Ashleigh glared at him. "How would he know?"

Dean licked his lips, his eyes never leaving the carcass. "He's a cop. Said there was a wild animal hoarder living out here in the woods, some rich guy, and he shot himself and let all the animals loose years ago, and they caught all the animals except a panther. And it's been out here ever since."

"That happened in Ohio," Ashleigh informed him. "Do you know how many people have looked for Perry? Hundreds, maybe thousands. And nobody has ever found any evidence of a panther living in Perrysville, Virginia."

"She's right," Connor said. "But there are clearly bears and coyotes. And if we don't want to be bear treats, we should get to the asylum before it gets dark." He glanced at the sky and Ashleigh did the same. The blue was more gray now, dusk creeping in around them.

"It's not far, now," she assured them, and went back to retrieve her box.

She was right in that it wasn't much further. But the rest of the walk was harrowing. Creatures were coming alive in the twilight all around them, and Kayla jumped and squeaked and clung to Dean every time a branch snapped or a bush rustled. The tension was so tight it was like an over-tuned guitar string, ready to snap.

Finally, something made a sound in the descending evening, something animal, something close to a wolf's howl but also not, the sound rougher and oozing malice. Ashleigh's body twitched at the sound, her nerves burning as if they were lit with matches.

"What is that?" Dean asked.

Her nerves thrumming, Ashleigh tried to sound confident and unafraid. "Coyotes."

"Coyotes don't sound like that," Kayla whimpered.

The howl faded and then started again, louder and even more malicious this time. Kayla ran, dropping her bags and scrambling pell-mell up the mountainside. Her fear was contagious, and the others followed in a mad dash for safety. Ashleigh ran with the box still towed behind her, but she could feel it getting stuck, bouncing, tearing, water bottles spinning away into the underbrush. She told herself she'd go back for them later, in the light, when it was safe.

The asylum reared up before them so suddenly it felt as if it had been lurking in the trees, waiting for the most dramatic moment to make an entrance.

"Where's the door?" Kayla screamed, slapping her hands against the cement overgrown with vines and moss.

"Here, here!" Connor called. He raised one long leg and kicked out with one huge foot. Glass smashed against the sole of his sneaker. He threw the laptop bag he carried in through the broken window and followed it with his body.

Ashleigh wanted to yell for him to stop. There was a door here somewhere, they just had to find it. This was no way to enter their new home. It felt wrong and her flesh crawled as if in warning. She was too late, though. Connor had already breached the asylum's skin, and the others were following him.

Ashleigh looked back at her makeshift sled. The box was shredded. The trash bag had burst open and a few articles of her clothing stuck to the sides of the box. With a sigh, she went to retrieve them, but then she heard that sound again.

That inhuman howl. That terrible, husky wailing that made her lizard brain think about death, about disembowelment, about being something's food. The coyote's black and bloated insides swam into her mind's eye, her nose filling with the stench of decay.

She ran for the shelter the asylum provided, empty-handed and shaking.

Chapter 4

The asylum stank of rot and damp and something else, something sharp and pungent that made Ashleigh's nose hairs curl. Dozens of pairs of reflective eyes watched them from doorways and window sills, reflecting the dying sunlight back to them, shiny coins in the darkness.

"It smells like cat piss in here," Kayla said. She squealed as she almost stepped on a mysterious lump. She bent at the waist to inspect it. "Is that a bird?"

"Jesus fucking Christ," Connor muttered, looking around, his flashlight beam bouncing off mold-covered walls and piles of tiny, clean-picked skeletons.

"Ash, didn't you say this place would be abandoned?" Dean asked, his voice low.

Ashleigh frowned. "It is. Abandoned by people, anyway. I had no idea it would be full of cats though." She stepped gingerly around a pile of something she suspected might be literal shit. "It's not like I got to scout it out before we came here."

She fought the feeling of shame that rose in her gut. This had been her idea; she had brought her friends here. It was dark outside, and dark inside, and they had nowhere to sleep except on piles of stinking excrement and small rotting corpses, and also there were snakes and mangled coyotes and something that might be a bear howling just outside. So far, her brilliant idea was turning out to be a nightmare.

At least the howl had stopped. Or maybe they just couldn't hear it inside the asylum's thick concrete walls. Neither idea was comforting, and Ashleigh shivered.

"What do we do now?" Dean asked, eyes on her.

Ashleigh hated that he was asking her. She had to have all the ideas. She had to find all their squats, make sure they were empty, organize the move, find furniture, and generally do all the thinking and decision-making. And now, of course, now that one of her ideas had turned out to be terrible, now was the time they finally turned to her for leadership.

Connor beat her to the punch. "Maybe if we go upstairs there are some places the cats haven't gotten to."

Ashleigh nodded and looked away from Dean's accusatory stare.

"We should go home," Kayla said. She was hugging herself in the corner, staring out the wide picture windows at the rapidly darkening landscape.

"Tomorrow morning we can consider our options," Connor told her.

"We should go *now*."

"It's getting dark," Dean said with a shrug. "It's not safe."

"We should go *now*," Kayla repeated. Her voice was soft, and she spoke matter-of-factly, as if there could be no debate. "The mountain tried to warn us, to protect us, to stop us from coming here, but we just kept going. If we don't go now, we might not make it 'til morning."

"Don't be so dramatic," Connor said, his posture tensing.

"Don't do that shit," Kayla snapped at him, her demeanor changing in an instant. "You can do that shit to Ashleigh if she wants to put up with it, but don't do that to me."

"Dean," Connor barked, "see to your woman before I do."

Dean quickly hustled Kayla out of the room with his arms around her. Ashleigh and Connor stood in the lobby of the asylum—so much like the lobby of a hotel, Ashleigh thought—listening to Dean and Kayla arguing in sharp whispers. Connor was still carrying the giant stick, and he used it to push the detritus on the floor into a corner while they waited.

Ashleigh swayed in place. She was suddenly hyper-aware of every ache in her body, and they were too numerous to count. When was the last time she had eaten? She wouldn't be able to remain standing much longer. "I'm going upstairs," she said, and turned for the stairs.

Connor followed her without a word.

The pair made their way to the stairs and up, up and up to the second floor. Cats dashed out of their way by the dozen. Tiny bones and leaves and other unknown things crunched underfoot. This area had clearly been the dormitory. Connor opened the first closed door to reveal a wooden bed with a plastic-wrapped mattress, a bedside table, a lamp, and a little rug, black with mold. Everything was dusty as hell but otherwise untouched by their feline roommates, thanks to the closed door.

Ashleigh entered the room and flopped down on the mattress. A cloud of dust rose around her, making her eyes burn, and the smell of mold permeated her nostrils. She didn't care. Exhaustion made her limbs so very heavy. She just needed to lie down for a bit.

Connor squeezed her shoulder. "I'll go see what else I can find. You rest a while."

Ashleigh didn't even have the energy to nod. She heard Connor's footsteps grow faint as he moved down the hallway. Distantly, Kayla's high-pitched shouts and Dean's lower replies drifted through the quiet asylum. Somewhere, a cat yowled briefly before falling silent.

Safe from snakes and cats and arguing friends, Ashleigh let sleep suck her down into its warm, velvety embrace.

Sometime later, someone lifted her into his arms. She cracked her eyes enough to see that it was still dark. The scent of Connor's deodorant surrounded her and she relaxed into his arms.

He laid her down on a mattress and covered her with some kind of fabric. She tried not to think about it too hard so she wouldn't wake up completely. She felt her shoes being pulled from her feet, and then Connor joined her on the mattress. His arms wrapped around her, and in the safety of his embrace, she slept.

She dreamed of cats. Big, black cats and dead birds with eyeless skulls, making that horrible sound, that rasping howl that made her bones vibrate with the wrongness of it.

Chapter 5

Morning came too early. The sunlight was diffused by the dusty unwashed windows, but it was still too bright, and outside, birds belted out arias.

"Fucking birds," Connor groaned. "It's October. Shouldn't they be dying or something?"

Not for the first time, Ashleigh reminded herself she didn't love Connor for his brains. Her bladder hurt, and she reluctantly rolled from his grasp. "Gotta pee," she told him. She stood on unsteady legs, her calves aching from the previous day's climb. She took in the sight of the place where she'd slept the night before: a pile of mattresses in a community room. The doors to enter were decorated with stained glass that cast pretty, colorful shapes onto the dirty floor. The room held couches, probably crawling with mold and bugs, as well as side tables, coffee tables, lamps, and an old CRT television, all of which Connor had pushed out of the way to make their mattress piles. He'd covered her with a ratty afghan that only smelled faintly of mold.

"There's a bathroom over there," Dean said.

"Does the water work?" Ashleigh asked, unable to keep the hope from her voice.

Dean chuckled. "No, of course not, but the pipes are still there. Pissed in the sink this morning, myself."

"How is she going to piss in the sink, dumbass?" Connor asked.

"There's a shower," Dean answered.

Ashleigh wasn't sure she could hold it much longer and hurried to the bathroom. She peed, barefoot, standing up in the dry shower, which was a strange sensation if ever she'd felt one. It was lucky the room had a small window, or she would have been peeing in the dark, too.

When she emerged from the bathroom, everyone was sitting up. Connor stretched, showing off his biceps and triceps and his lean, muscular forearms. God, she loved his arms. They made her think all sorts of lascivious thoughts. Her mouth was dry and she grabbed a water bottle from the floor, only to find it empty.

"Someone should get the rest of the water from the car," she said.

"That's my lady, all business first thing in the morning," Connor joked, grabbing her around the waist and pressing his face to her belly. He breathed deeply and locked his arms around her.

"Sorry to care so much about whether we die up here."

Connor squeezed tighter. "I don't think we're going to die right this second.

"It takes three days to die of dehydration, so I guess we've got a little time." With a sigh of resignation, Ashleigh wrapped her arms around him and leaned into a kiss.

"She's right though," Dean said, standing up and pulling on jeans over his boxers. He was so thin he had to cinch his belt tight to keep the jeans on his bony hips. "I'll go back to the car with you, Ash."

"I want to go," Kayla said. Her voice was thick with sleep and congestion, from the dust or from crying, or maybe both. "But I'm not coming back. I'm getting out of here. Y'all can come with me if you want."

Silence fell over the group. Connor pulled Ashleigh into his lap and buried his face in her hair.

Dean sat beside Kayla and took her hand. "I know you want to go back, but we can't go back with you, Kay. Me and Connor are wanted men."

"You're just going to leave us here, without a car," Connor said, his tone resentful. Beneath Ashleigh's hands, his muscles tightened.

"It's my car, and I didn't want to come out here in the first place," Kayla said, not making eye contact with any of them. "You can come to the car to get the rest of your stuff, but then I'm leaving." She stood and forced her feet into her shoes. Then she hesitated, staring down at Dean. "I wish you'd come with me. It's not safe here." Her gaze moved to Ashleigh.

Ashleigh, fully enveloped in Connor's arms, his breath hot against her neck, couldn't imagine leaving him. "It's a lot less scary in the daytime. I think we were just panicking over that weird sound, and that was probably just the wind. The place needs to be cleaned up, sure, but that's nothing a little elbow grease won't solve."

Kayla frowned and shook her head. "Fine. It's your funeral. Let's get out of here."

Dean and Connor stood, reluctantly. "You coming, babe?" Connor asked Ashleigh.

She shook her head. "My legs are killing me. And you're stronger than I am, anyway. You won't need me."

"But I'll miss you." He stuck out his lower lip in a child-like pout.

Ashleigh grinned. "Absence makes the heart grow fonder. Besides, I can poke around looking for more stuff we can use, and maybe even start cleaning up a little."

Connor grinned his most mischievous grin, his eyes twinkling. "That does sound like women's work."

"Sexist pig!" Ashleigh playfully slugged his arm.

He stood, throwing her over his shoulder in one smooth motion. "Sorry, I couldn't hear you, your voice is too small and girly!"

Ashleigh screamed and giggled as he carried her around the room, chanting about how he was a big strong man and she needed him to do all the heavy lifting. Finally she grabbed the waistband of his boxers and pulled. He howled and dropped her onto the mattresses.

"A wedgie? Really? That's so sixth grade," Connor said, groaning and pulling the fabric from between his butt cheeks. "I'm gonna get you back for that!" He glanced at Dean and Kayla, waiting by the door. "But later." He winked, kissed her one last time, and went out the door.

Ashleigh laid back on the pile of mattresses Connor had made the night before, listening to her friends' footsteps as they made their way to the exit. He'd done a pretty good job making them a comfortable place to sleep. This room was very clean, except for the dust, and the bathroom was close. He'd placed the flashlight within arm's reach, and now she grabbed it, pulled on her sneakers, and decided to go see what she could find that might be useful.

She opened the door and cats scattered in every direction. The smell of ammonia and rot hit her so hard she gagged and retreated back into the community room for a few seconds before attempting to exit again. This time, it didn't seem as pungent. But, she thought, Kayla was probably right. They shouldn't stay here. Who knew what damage to their lungs the cat piss and mold would do, long-term.

Of course, it probably wasn't anything worse than what crystal had already done to their bodies. This was still their best chance to get clean. It's not like they could go to a rehab on the beach, though she suspected her dad might offer to pay for rehab one more time if she could convince him she was really sure she didn't want to use anymore. That would be a nice vacation. Certainly nicer than this.

But they would make her give up Connor, the one thing she couldn't bring herself to do.

Gripping Connor's flashlight, she ascended to the second floor. More cats skittered away, except for a big orange tomcat. He watched her from a windowsill, his eyes narrowed, his expression unreadable. He had no interest in giving her the right of way. This was *his* asylum. She was just an annoying visitor, and he wouldn't be scared off by some tourist.

The third floor was another dormitory floor, room after room of beds and dressers and rotten carpets. Ashleigh found a few towels that weren't completely moldy and a few blankets that seemed serviceable. An abandoned sweater waited for her in one of the rooms, the kind that looked like maybe an old man had worn it while he smoked a pipe, and Ashleigh pulled it on. If it had an odor, she couldn't smell it over everything else in this rank place.

At the other end of the building was another community room. A few crumbling paperback books had been left behind, and a broken sofa. Ashleigh carried the sofa's cushions back to the nest of mattresses on the second floor. She had to make three trips to get them all.

The tomcat watched her from the windowsill as she carried her treasures downstairs. "I know, I know," she said to him. "All this stuff is probably haunted." She sneezed, nearly dropping the disintegrating books clutched under one arm.

She paused after her final trip and went to a window, wiping the dust away with one sweater sleeve. Outside, the yellow and orange forest stretched away from the asylum and down the rolling hills to Perrysville. The view was lovely, the sky blue and the sunlight golden in the way it only ever was in October. Perrysville looked quaint from this distance. Quaint and abandoned, as she was too far away to make out any people. Cars scooted around the roads like Hot Wheels pushed around by a giant, invisible hand. She liked the idea of Perrysville without any people. That would be an improvement.

It felt like Kayla and the boys had been gone a long time, but they had to go all the way to the car and back, which was at least two hours of walking. Ashleigh checked her cell phone for the time, but she wasn't sure what time they had left. That was a perk of asylum living, she supposed. She wouldn't need to know what time it was, or even what day of the week, without a job to go to or appointments to keep. She could let go of a lot of stress. Of course, there were other stresses, like what the fuck to do about all these fucking cats.

Her cell phone was going to die eventually, and she had zero bars out here anyway, but that was another sort of luxury, wasn't it? Completely cut off from the real world, even Candy Crush Saga. They could really reset themselves up here. Celebrities paid thousands for vacation retreats like this. Well, not *exactly* like this.

Ashleigh cupped her hands against the glass and looked toward the overgrown road to the asylum. The grass swayed in the breeze, undisturbed. Probably Connor and Dean were just taking their time walking back. Maybe they were gathering all the clothes and water bottles she'd dropped during their mad dash to the asylum last night.

She decided to investigate the basement and went to the stairs. A dozen cats watched her from the floor below, sitting so placidly that only their huge, gleaming, round eyes gave away their alertness. Their stares were unnerving, but they fled as Ashleigh started to descend. Was it normal for a colony to have so many cats? Ashleigh didn't know much about cats and even less about stray or feral ones, so she just didn't know. But it sure seemed like a *lot* of cats. She wasn't sure there were this many cats in Perrysville, even if you visited every single home and counted them all.

The smell of cat piss intensified as she descended into the basement until she had to pull the sweater over her mouth and nose. The flashlight revealed innumerable carcasses and turds in the basement hallway. A few cats crouched at the end of the hall, their eyes reflecting the flashlight beam. Ashleigh's eyes watered and she thought about turning back. She had come this far, though. There could be some good stuff hiding down here if she could find a storage room.

The first door she came across swung open to reveal an office. A heavy wooden desk sat in the middle of the floor, with a metal rolling chair behind it. There were tall wooden bookshelves but they were empty. The ceiling was the sort of drop ceiling used in offices that wanted to hide the pipes and wires above. Ashleigh used her finger to write her name on the thick layer of dust coating the desktop, in cursive that would have made her fourth-grade teacher proud.

The next room was locked. The sign on the door said RECORDS. Ashleigh wondered if there were still actual records behind the door, or if they had been moved. Back when this asylum had been in use, they would have kept records on paper in filing cabinets and she had a strong feeling they had been left behind with other heavy items—like the oak desk—when the asylum was abandoned. She pressed her hand against the cool wooden door and decided not to mention this room to Connor. He would want to pick the lock or break the door down and start pulling files, looking for identities to steal. Somehow this room felt sacred to her, filled as it was with sensitive information, the kind nobody would ever want anyone to know about themselves or their loved ones. It didn't feel right to invade the privacy of sick people, even if many of them were probably dead by now.

The next door was far down the long hallway. Her soft, sneakered footsteps seemed incredibly loud in the silence. The door creaked when she opened it, an ominous sound that reminded her of the horror movies she'd loved watching with her mom—when she was sober—with an unexpected pang of emotion.

The flashlight beam illuminated a chair in the middle of the room. It was metal and bolted to the floor. Leather cuffs were attached where wrists and ankles would have been when someone sat in the chair. Beside it, there was a small silver cart, the kind surgeons use for their surgical tools while they work. This cart was empty, though.

Ashleigh removed the sweater from her face and shut the door, inhaling air that smelled only faintly of metal and must. The flashlight beam found cabinets against the back wall, and a long metal table.

She inspected the chair. Like the creaking door, it was something out of a horror movie. Had people been given electroshock therapy in this room? Had their organs been stolen by sinister doctors to sell on the black market? Or were they forced to watch videos with their eyes held open by cold metal instruments, unable to blink?

Ashleigh laughed at herself even though her chest was tight with fear. These were all images from movies, probably deeply inaccurate ones. She was just scaring herself. She took a few deep breaths to calm her fluttering heart and opened the nearest cabinet. It contained a few vials of discolored liquid and two boxes of surgical gloves. She tucked the boxes of gloves under her free arm but left the vials. The other cabinets were empty.

The sense of being watched crept up Ashleigh's neck. She gasped, whirling to shine the flashlight beam at the doorway, but it was empty.

Thump thump thump. The sound of footsteps came from above her. At first, she reasoned that Connor and Dean must have returned. But, somehow, the longer she listened to the irregular thumps, the more she became convinced they didn't sound right. They didn't sound human. Breathing hard, she tipped her head back and lifted the flashlight to shine it at the drop ceiling. Movement in the corner caught her attention and she pointed the light at it even as her limbic system wailed at her to run, to get out of this room. Survival was more important than knowing what might be there, but even so, her feet were locked in place and her eyes searched the darkness.

The beam of light pierced the corner without the interruption of the ceiling. There were missing tiles. The darkness seemed denser there, and it moved, an impossible undulation that made panic rise in Ashleigh's throat.

She screamed, dropped the gloves, and ran for the door, slamming it behind her. She dashed up the stairs to the first floor. Hissing cats fled her path and tiny skeletons crunched under her sneakers. She didn't stop running until she arrived outside in the sunlight, where the brightness felt like it could scour away the last shreds of darkness that clung to her.

Chapter 6

Kayla stared at Ashleigh from where she sat on a chunk of concrete. She was frozen in motion, a cigarette clasped between her fingers, halfway to her mouth. The skin around her eyes was puffy and red, and her right knee bounced a quick, nervous rhythm. "You okay?"

Ashleigh took a second to catch her breath. She nodded and grunted, "What are you doing here? I thought you weren't coming back."

Kayla frowned and took a drag. "Car's tires are slashed."

Ashleigh felt all the heat drain from her face. "What?"

"Yeah. Can't leave until I can find someplace with a signal and call for help."

"How did the tires get slashed? Nobody knows we're here."

Kayla shot her a look and said, "Except that clearly someone does."

"That doesn't make any sense. There aren't any homes or businesses up here." The sensation of panic thrummed behind Ashleigh's breastbone and her vision started to narrow again. "Where are the guys?"

"Collecting all the shit we dropped on the way here. I carried what I could." Kayla nodded to a trash bag dumped on the ground next to the door. "Guys have the rest." She took another drag and exhaled the smoke through her nose before asking, "What's going on with you?"

Ashleigh crouched beside Kayla and gulped a few deep breaths. She shook her head and swallowed down the jittery feeling until it was a cold stone in her belly. "I thought I saw something. Couldn't have been real though. Shadows don't move on their own."

Kayla's eyes grew huge. "Hallucinating already? Seems early for that. Not that I know anything about withdrawal."

"What about hallucinating?" Connor and Dean appeared, laden with bags and boxes. They'd stuffed water bottles in their pockets, making their pants sag, so they both walked with a curious wide-legged gait.

Ashleigh ran to Connor and threw her arms around him. He dropped what he was carrying and hugged her back. "Whoa, babe, you okay?"

"I thought I saw something in the basement," she gasped.

"You went down there by yourself?" Connor asked.

"Yeah, of course. Why not? I'm a big girl."

Connor kissed the top of her head. "No more exploring alone, okay?"

She nodded against his chest.

"Find anything good?" Dean asked, placing his bags on the ground and reaching for Kayla's cigarette.

"A few things," Ashleigh said.

"And some hallucinations," Kayla added.

Smoke poured from Kayla's mouth when she spoke, giving Ashleigh unpleasant memories of her mother, drunk and smoking in the living room in her underwear, some naked man sleeping it off in her bed. Ashleigh shivered so hard her teeth clacked together.

"When was the last time you ate?" Connor asked her.

Dean dug in his pack and pulled out two boxes of snack cakes. "What does the lady prefer, Twinkies or Ding Dongs?"

Ashleigh accepted a Twinkie, admitting to herself that low blood sugar could cause hallucinations. It had never happened to her before, but it was possible, especially under this much stress. Especially when detoxing.

She chewed and swallowed a couple of snack cakes and drank a few gulps of bottled water. She didn't really taste any of it. Her eyes were drawn to the blacked-over basement windows while she ate. They reflected less light than the other windows, like a void. She shuddered, remembering the thumps of footsteps over her head and the movement of the shadows in the corner of the room, like a sinuous black snake lashing.

It was just her imagination, she reassured herself, letting the sun warm her skin. She felt better already now that Connor was back. Everything was going to be okay.

Chapter 7

After their quick meal, Kayla stood and took out her cellphone. "There's no fucking signal," she huffed bitterly.

Ashleigh pulled out her phone and nodded to the slope on the other side of the asylum. "Maybe if we get higher we can find some bars."

Kayla nodded. "Good idea." She got up, her expression giving away nothing, and walked away, holding her phone aloft and watching it for bars. Ashleigh jumped up and followed her but kept her phone in her pocket. If they ran the batteries down, their only chance to charge their phones would be in the car. The car with the slashed tires. And that would only last for as long as there was gas in the tank.

Once they had moved away from the guys, Ashleigh asked Kayla if she was okay. "You seem…numb."

Kayla shrugged. "Yeah, I guess crying for hours will do that to a person."

"Because of the slashed tires?" Ashleigh's words came out stilted as she struggled up the steep incline.

"Mostly."

"How do you think the tires got wrecked?"

"How should I know?"

"Are you sure they were slashed?"

Kayla let out a bark of acidic laughter. "Ask the guys if you don't believe me."

Ashleigh pressed her lips together in frustration. "I do believe you. I'm trying to ask if they could have been slashed unintentionally. By like...I dunno...deer antlers or something."

Kayla chortled. "That's imaginative."

"What did the rest of the car look like?"

Kayla paused, looking back and frowning down at her. "Like a car. What's with the interrogation?"

"Look, I wasn't there to see it. I'm just trying to get more information."

Kayla put her eyes back on her phone and moved forward again. "I don't know why you would need more information. There's someone out here who doesn't want us to leave. They slashed my tires. The end."

"Why would they do that?"

"Do you really want my theory?" Kayla asked.

Ashleigh wasn't sure she did, but she said yeah anyway.

"There's a murderer living out here and we're all going to end up looking like that coyote on the road. That's why I'm over here frantically looking for a phone signal. Don't you have Verizon?"

Ashleigh confirmed she did.

"You'll probably have a better chance of finding a signal than me."

Ashleigh pulled out her phone and turned it on. She held it up. They had walked maybe a hundred yards from the asylum, up a steep slope. One bar flickered to life. "I've got it!" Her fingers pressed the button to dial her dad automatically. "It's ringing!"

"Who are you calling?" Kayla asked, staring at Ashleigh's phone wide-eyed, her free hand twitching.

Ashleigh didn't answer. She waited breathlessly as the phone rang in her ear, the connection full of static. The time in between rings seemed to stretch out interminably. After the fourth ring, a familiar voice answered, "Hello?"

"Dad?"

"Hello?"

"Dad, it's me, it's Ashleigh. I need your help!"

"Hello? Is someone there? I can barely hear you."

Ashleigh's heart clenched so tight that when she tried to speak again, the only sound she made was a desperate wheeze.

"Please call me back from another phone." The call disconnected, and Ashleigh lowered the phone from her ear.

"He couldn't hear me," she told Kayla.

"Goddammit," Kayla growled. She whirled and resumed marching up the slope.

Slipping her phone back into her pocket, Ashleigh followed. She didn't speak anymore, as her throat was full with a painful lump.

They spent hours walking this way and that, trying to find a signal, but had no luck. Finally, frustrated and thirsty, they turned back to the asylum.

Dean crouched over a small fire on the concrete patio. He'd swept away the leaves to make a spot safe for a fire and surrounded his makeshift fire pit with chunks of concrete and rocks. A thin shaft of smoke rose into the blue sky. Ashleigh felt like her hopes were going with it.

"Any luck?" he asked.

Both women shook their heads despondently. "I'm going to lie down," Kayla said, and disappeared into the asylum.

Ashleigh plopped down in the grass beside Dean. He had a bottle of water in his pocket and she plucked it out and took a long drink. The water was warm and tasted stale. It was difficult to make herself swallow it, but she did.

Dean smiled at her, but it was an exhausted, sad smile. "We took the bags upstairs and saw all the stuff you found. Good job."

Ashleigh nodded. "I didn't explore the whole basement, though. Could be more down there."

"That's where you saw…"

"The hallucination, yeah."

Dean was silent for a few seconds while he stabbed at the fire with a stick. "What did it look like?"

Ashleigh shrugged, trying to seem nonchalant. She didn't really want to remember, but the image of the scintillating shadow oozed across her mind. "Like the darkness moved. I was shining the flashlight right at it, but it didn't penetrate the shadows. And then they sort of…" She held up her arm and made an undulating movement.

Dean nodded and frowned. "Don't tell Kayla, okay?"

"She already knows."

"Dammit, she's scared enough already, Ash."

"Yeah. She told me she thinks there's a killer out here who's trying to keep us from leaving."

Dean sighed. "It's either that or Perry the fucking Panther has it out for us."

"You really think there's someone out here slashing our tires so he can murder us?"

"Can you come up with a better explanation?"

Ashleigh frowned and stared into the flames. "No."

An uneasy silence settled over them. In the forest, birds chirped and squirrels chittered. Something screeched and the wind made the trees rustle. Chilled, Ashleigh thrust her hands in her sleeves. The sweater she'd found was ugly and scratchy but it sure was warm.

Connor emerged from the front door without warning. "What are you two chatting about, all friendly-like?"

Ashleigh realized she was sitting very close to Dean so she could drink his water and talk to him in a near-whisper. She scooted away from him immediately. "We didn't find a signal," she said.

Connor sniffed. "Kayla told me." As if on cue, Kayla stepped out of the shadows.

Dean put a couple of sticks on the fire. "Man, what I wouldn't give for a fix."

Ashleigh licked her lips. Meth would be nice, right now, but she didn't want to admit it. After all, they were here partially to get clean, at her insistence. She would have to be the strong one.

Connor reached into his pocket and pulled out a baggie of familiar blue-white shards.

"What the fuck, Connor. We came out here to get clean." There was no intensity behind her words. Ashleigh wanted to be angry, wanted to shout at him and rage and throw the baggie of crystals into the fire, or, even better, run off with it into the woods and bury it.

But she didn't, because that baggie looked so good. She could almost smell the crystal-laced smoke, almost taste it on her tongue. Everything difficult would be so much easier if she could just smoke her concerns away.

"Just one last time, babe. A farewell smoke. You wouldn't want to waste it, would you?"

She looked at Kayla and Dean for support, but they were practically salivating, staring at Connor like he was the second coming. And she had to admit, after what had happened in the basement, she could use a hit to calm her nerves. Maybe this would be the sendoff they needed before quitting cold-turkey, anyway. This way, they wouldn't feel cheated. They could enjoy crystal one last time and give it up knowing they had enjoyed it to the fullest.

They lit up right there outside the asylum's front doors. It felt less blasphemous, somehow, than lighting up inside. Connor took the first hit and passed it to Ashleigh, who gave it to Dean, who passed it to Kayla. Kayla had trouble working the lighter, and Dean had to help her.

Ashleigh sighed with pleasure as the smoke entered her lungs and the familiar feeling of euphoria washed over her almost instantly. All the pain, doubt, fear, and weariness in her body seemed to flee at one time. They would be back, though, if she didn't keep smoking. The flute came around again and again, and each time she took a hit, the sense of lightness was stronger. She had so much energy she got up and paced. Her legs wanted her to run through the long grass, churning and pumping to expel the bright light that threatened to burst from her body.

Kayla moaned and Ashleigh looked over to see Dean had pulled up her shirt and was suckling her left nipple. Where was Connor? Ashleigh wanted him to do that to her. She wanted to feel *everything*.

She found him staring wide-eyed at the trees. "The trees are trying to tell me something," he said. "I don't know what it is though."

Ashleigh took his hand and placed it on her tit. "We should go fuck." She gestured at their friends.

Connor didn't need to be asked twice. He grabbed her and carried her into the asylum. She squealed and wrapped her legs around his waist. The building breathed around them, walls heaving like the movement of lungs. Cats peeked at them from around corners, eyes shining.

He led her to one of the first-floor examination rooms and began kissing her, his warm mouth moving from her lips to her jaw to her neck. Her shirt came away like the peel of a fruit. She climbed out of her jeans and panties, relishing the feeling of the cool air on her skin. God, it felt good to be naked. Why did they even bother wearing clothes? Especially up here, where no one could see them. She wanted to feel like this all the time, naked and free, her skin tingling with need.

Connor took another hit from the flute and gave it to her. She lit the last tiny bit of crystal and sucked down more smoke greedily. The tingling intensified, her need for him unfurling like a velvet rose, blood red and unimaginably intense, something she could hardly contain. Her skin was so hot with desire it wanted to blister and flay itself from her body.

She lay back on the examination table and spread herself for him. Connor lowered himself on top of her, licking and sucking and biting, and then the sweet bliss of him between her legs. She needed him so much, needed him to be inside her, needed the exquisite pressure of him. She moaned, the sensations so overwhelming they drove her to the edge of darkness, the edge of reason. She was made of liquid pleasure that writhed and whimpered.

They had left the door to the examination room open just a sliver. A shadow stood there in the gap, eyes fixed on Ashleigh as Connor thrust himself in and out of her in the twilight of the examination room. In a haze of ecstasy, she extended her arm, beckoning to the new addition to join them. The shadow moved a little closer to the door, and its eyes were bright green, like iridescent butterfly wings or gently glowing bioluminescent algae.

"Who are you?" Ashleigh breathed, her voice full of wonder.

Chapter 8

Connor looked over his shoulder and issued a shout when he saw the shadow. His body tensed and he withdrew from her, rushing to the door, throwing it open, and running out into the hallway. He shouted with fury, struggling to yank his jeans over his hips and run at the same time.

Ashleigh hopped off the table and took her time redressing herself. She still longed for the release of an orgasm and disappointment was a heavy weight between her legs.

Connor roared outside, followed by Kayla shrieking, loud and long, a sound of horror. Ashleigh slid her feet into her shoes and ran for the door.

Dean was on the ground and Connor was kicking him. Kayla, topless, sobbed and battered at Connor with useless fists.

Panic lanced through Ashleigh, dissolving the haze of meth and lust. "What are you doing?"

"He was watching us, the little shit," Connor barked, kicking Dean in the gut. Dean didn't even try to defend himself, just curled into a ball and tried to protect his vital organs. It was pathetic. Ashleigh kind of wanted to kick him herself for being such a wimp, but instead she grabbed Connor's arm and hauled him away with all her strength.

"It wasn't him," she shouted.

Connor stopped kicking their friend and turned to her. "What?"

Kayla threw herself over Dean protectively, wailing.

"It wasn't him," Ashleigh repeated. "Watching us. It wasn't Dean."

"It couldn't have been Dean," Kayla screamed, her mouth twisted into an ugly shape. "He was out here with me the whole time."

Connor paled. "Then who was it?"

Ashleigh shook her head. "I don't know. I couldn't see. It was just a shadow."

No one spoke for a few seconds. Dean groaned and Kayla wept. And then Connor said, "Does that mean there's someone else here?"

"We were high. Maybe I imagined it," Ashleigh said.

"I saw him, too." Connor looked down at Dean. "It had to be Dean."

"It wasn't me, man," Dean said, pushing himself up to kneel. He spat blood onto the grass. "Me and Kayla were out here the whole time. Why you always gotta kick *me*, man?" Tears glimmered in his eyes as he stared up at Connor. "Why is it always me?"

Connor ignored him. "Then someone else is already living here. In the asylum."

"Who would live here?" Ashleigh demanded. "It's filthy. It smells like cat shit. No sane person would do that."

"We're doing it," Kayla rasped, getting to her feet. "Maybe someone else had the same idea as us. Free shelter, off the grid, where the cops can't find you. Maybe he's been here, waiting for people like us, and now he's going to pick us off one by one, just like *I told you*." Her voice increased in volume and pitch as she spoke until she was screaming.

"Don't be ridiculous," Connor said, just as Ashleigh said, "This isn't a slasher movie."

Dean struggled to stand and put a hand on Kayla's arm. "Kay, don't worry. There's nobody here. They were seeing things. Remember that time we were high and we thought we saw Totoro at the bus stop?"

Kayla crossed her arms over her chest and shook, eyes wide, fat tears running down her cheeks.

Ashleigh grabbed Kayla's shirt off the ground and handed it to her. "He had big green eyes, like shiny green eyes, so it was probably just one of the cats."

"A cat the size of Dean?" Kayla asked, her voice a tremulous squeak. She took the shirt and dressed herself.

"No, just a regular cat," Ashleigh said quickly. She looked at Connor for help.

Connor sighed. "Yeah. It was definitely just a fucking cat." He glared at Dean.

Ashleigh rolled her eyes. "C'mon, Kayla, I think you had a bad trip. I'll take you upstairs so you can sleep it off."

Kayla shook her head and took a step back. "Not alone. I'm not going in there alone."

"We'll all go," Dean said, placing his arms around his girlfriend and guiding her to the door. "You won't be alone."

Together, the four of them trundled up the stairs to the community room. Now that her high had worn off, Ashleigh was conscious of every ache and itch, and she had a lot of them. She scratched at her scalp and wished for a shower. She lay awake on the mattress for a long time in only her panties and t-shirt, staring at the cracked concrete ceiling, listening to the others breathing heavily, birds or bats fluttering their wings, cats hissing and yowling at each other. She had expected this place to be quieter than their squat in the suburbs, but it had a life of its own she was getting used to. Eventually the asylum's weird lullaby put her to sleep.

She dreamed she was strapped down in the metal chair in the basement. Blood gushed from between her legs, filling the room with the smell of hot iron. A doctor wearing a mask that concealed his face knelt between her knees. He held up a pair of rusty tongs and clacked them twice. He said something, but Ashleigh couldn't hear him over the sound of her own screams.

"Baby, baby, shhhh, you're okay." Connor shook her awake and pulled her into his embrace. "It's just a nightmare."

Ashleigh's senses returned. She was in the community room, but it was darker than it had been earlier—it must be dusk. Connor was wrapped around her, the scent of him surrounding her in a comforting cloud. Nearby, she could hear Dean snoring softly, sleeping the sleep of the dead, as he always did after a fix.

"You okay?" He looked into her eyes with surprising tenderness, one hand caressing her jaw.

Ashleigh burrowed into his chest, fighting back tears. "I'm okay. I have nightmares sometimes, after we smoke."

"I know. But that seemed…worse than usual." Connor stroked her hair. He was naked except for his boxers, his lean, muscular body pressed against hers.

Ashleigh was suddenly very aware that she was wearing only a flimsy t-shirt and a pair of old, threadbare panties. She should have been aroused by his nearness, but instead she could only think about the stench of blood, the crimson ocean that had poured from between her legs in the dream, and the *clack clack* of the faceless doctor's filthy tongs. Connor was incredibly warm, so warm it made her feel like she was overheating. Nausea made her stomach lurch.

She pushed against him, trying to free herself.

Connor gripped her tighter. His erection pressed against her thigh. He kissed her forehead and nibbled on her earlobe. The awful sucking sound his mouth made in her ear made Ashleigh cringe.

"No, Connor. Not right now."

"Come on, baby. We didn't finish what we started earlier." He leaned in and pressed his mouth against hers, his lips and tongue writhing.

Ashleigh didn't return the kiss. She pressed against his chest with her hands and turned her head away so his mouth landed on her cheek. "No, Connor. I just had a nightmare. I don't feel like it."

"Ashleigh, baby, come on. You know it hurts my feelings when you say no, and I'm still hard from earlier. It hurts."

With a grunt of effort, Ashleigh brought up her knee into his groin, crushing his most sensitive parts. "I bet that hurts more."

Connor shouted and released her, rolling away with his hands between his legs. "You bitch," he gasped.

Ashleigh jumped up and ran to the pile of her clothes the boys had rescued from the woods. She pulled out a pair of booty shorts and yanked them over her underwear. While Connor groaned and his face turned purple, she slid her feet into her shoes and bolted from the room and down the stairs, the stairs that suddenly seemed impossibly long, her footsteps so loud pounding down each step she imagined people could hear them in Perrysville. She flew out the door of the asylum, frantic, knowing that Connor would be behind her any second, full of fury.

Kayla poked absent-mindedly at Dean's little fire. "Ashleigh?"

Ashleigh ran past, headed for the trees, saying only, "Connor's angry."

"Oh, god, Ash," Kayla called after her. "What did you do?"

Chapter 9

Ashleigh hid in the woods, crouched under a log. Connor came out of the asylum, bellowing for her. Trembling, Ashleigh tunneled into the earth, pressing herself under the log as far as she could, her body squeezing down flat. Ants crawled across her limbs. A spider skittered across her face. She didn't allow herself to breathe, much less scream. Ants and spiders were far less dangerous than Connor's wrath. Hell, she might take a chance on a rattlesnake over the definite violence of her lover's rage.

A cat appeared, a small black one, probably a juvenile. It crouched and stared at Ashleigh with huge yellow eyes. It took a few steps toward her, the nostrils in its triangle-shaped nose sniffing. She thought it might come close enough for her to touch it, but it started at some sound Ashleigh couldn't hear and sped away into the trees.

She wondered if a part of her had always known it would come to this. Connor made her feel safe and cared for as long as she obeyed him. He wasn't really safe, though, not when he was so volatile. She had told herself for the last two years that she was the exception, and he would never turn his violent nature on her, but clearly she'd been naive. She was no exception. She felt like a fool. She ground her teeth in frustration.

But she couldn't live without him, could she? She had tried, and failed, twice. She'd have to go back to the asylum eventually, when he was calmer, and face the consequences for her actions. Maybe he would be forgiving. He did love her, after all. As much as a man like him could love. Besides, it wasn't safe, alone in the woods.

After a while, she heard Kayla's voice, higher and softer, in the gaps between Connor's shouts. She couldn't hear what Kayla said, but eventually Connor stopped shouting. The silence that followed made every hair on Ashleigh's body stand on end. Eventually the insects and birds that had silenced themselves during Connor's outburst began to make noise again, and the frantic pounding of her heart calmed.

Ashleigh waited a while, until darkness descended over the forest in earnest, until the cheerful chirps of daytime birds were replaced with the low, menacing hoots of owls, and then she slid out from under the log to brush the bugs and spiders from her body and shake them out of her hair. She crept through the trees, back to the asylum. She could hide in the basement until tomorrow. By then, Connor would be calm, and the danger would be past.

She tiptoed down the stairs and into the dark hallway. Without a flashlight, the basement was black like a starless night. She found her way by touch, the cement walls rough under her fingers. She couldn't see the cats in the darkness but she heard them, skittering, hissing, running. There was a sound, a rhythmic sound, a thumping and scraping. Ashleigh's heartbeat thrummed in time with the sound. She knew she should turn back, that the source of the sound couldn't possibly be good, but she kept walking. She was compelled, her feet moving without her command.

A thin ribbon of dim light glowed under one of the doorways. She knew what room it was. She knew the sounds that came from the other side—thumps, scrapes, the slap of flesh, and small, desperate cries. A painful stone rose in her throat and tears burned in her eyes. She didn't want to push the door open, but she did it anyway. She knew what she would see. She still had to look.

The flashlight had been placed on the floor so that it illuminated the room in a cone of bright white LED light. On the torture chair, Kayla knelt, naked from the waist down, clutching hard at the back of the chair, her face contorted. Connor stood behind her, hands gripping her hips, clothed but with his pants at his ankles, thrusting forward and pulling back, his head tipped back and eyes closed, groaning with each thrust. Kayla made little mewling sounds, rocking back and forth, meeting his thrusts. Their motions made fleshy slapping sounds in time with the chair scraping rhythmically against the floor.

They were both oblivious to the open door and Ashleigh watching them. She stood there for several seconds, fascinated, horrified, disgusted, hardly able to believe what she was seeing. And then it abruptly all crystallized in her mind, and what she was seeing felt strangely inevitable. The sense of confusion and amazement passed, leaving only the hot flush of rage.

She lunged forward, grabbed the long metal flashlight, and smashed it against Connor's skull. "You fucking bastard," she screamed, hitting him three times before he brought a hand up to ward against the unexpected attack. She saw blood on his temple just before the light went out, and she ran.

In a haze of fury and sorrow, she made her way down the hall, up the stairs, and to the community room that was bathed in moonlight. Dean snored on his back, his limbs in the shape of a starfish. Ashleigh didn't have to tell him, didn't have to break his heart, but she also couldn't bear this pain and horror alone, so she screamed his name until he roused.

"What's wrong?" Dean asked, sitting up, blinking sleep from his eyes.

"They're fucking in the basement," Ashleigh told him.

"Who?" Dean asked. She didn't answer, and his eyes widened as he realized who it had to be. "Kayla and Connor?" Connor's name came out a thick, choked sound. "No. That can't be right. They wouldn't do that to us."

"Of course they fucking would. Connor is an asshole and Kayla is an idiot. And they're both pissed at us." Ashleigh paced, swinging the heavy flashlight. Her hand hurt from gripping it so hard but she couldn't let go, like her fingers were locked in place permanently.

"You...you saw them?"

"Yes. Do you want all the sordid details? They were doing it doggy-style on a medical chair—"

"Oh god, no, please." Dean held up his hands to stop her. His voice cracked, and she realized he was crying.

The sound of footsteps on the stairs alerted them to visitors. Ashleigh moved away from the door just before it swung open to admit Kayla and then Connor.

"Dean..." Kayla said, running in. Her ponytail was crooked and her clothes were twisted.

"No, no," Dean moaned, rising to stand. He covered his face with his hands, as if he couldn't look at her.

Kayla turned to Ashleigh. "You told him?"

Ashleigh chortled. "Fuck yeah I did. He deserves to know his girlfriend is a cheating slut."

"I only did it because Connor was so angry at you," Kayla whined. "I did it so he wouldn't hurt you."

Ashleigh let out a bitter laugh. "I'm supposed to be *grateful* you fucked my boyfriend?"

Connor approached Ashleigh, his hands held palm up, like she was a rabid animal. Dark liquid trickled down his face from the gash by his temple. "Ash, you have no right to be angry. You kneed me in the fucking balls—"

She brandished the flashlight. "Don't fucking come near me. I saw you with her. I *saw you*. There's no explaining. There are no excuses. There's just you and her, getting the fuck out of here. I never want to see either of you ever again." It felt so good to be so angry. Ashleigh was a dragon, and she would destroy them all with fire.

"Why?" Dean cried, holding his head like it was going to explode and his hands were the only thing keeping his skull together. "Why did you do this? With *him*?"

Kayla stepped closer to Dean and said something Ashleigh couldn't hear.

Connor took another step toward Ashleigh and abruptly changed tactics, dropping to his knees. "Baby, I'm sorry. I was just frustrated and Kayla was there. I'm so sorry. This was the first time and the last time. You know how much I love you."

Ashleigh backed away from him, rage making her hot and shaky. For the first time in their whole relationship, she wasn't afraid of him. "Get out. I mean it! You can die out in the woods for all I care."

Dean pushed Kayla away from him. She fell on her ass. He moved so quickly he was a blur in the silver moonlight. He jumped on top of Connor. He didn't stand a chance against the bigger man, but it didn't matter. He was righteous fury, personified. Connor had finally pushed him too far.

Ashleigh made her move on Kayla, grabbed her by the ponytail and dragging her, kicking and twisting, out the door into the stinking hallway. Anger made Ashleigh so strong she thought she could lift a bus and drop it on Kayla's head, if only there had been one available.

"You can get the fuck out of here, bitch! Or I swear to god, I'll kill you myself." Ashleigh smacked Kayla in the jaw with the flashlight, just once, and left her sobbing on the floor.

Ashleigh went back into the community room. Connor and Dean grappled. Even in the moonlight, even with their size difference, it was difficult to make out which man was which. They were one mass of enraged flesh, kicking and punching, grunting and growling, feet slipping on the plastic mattresses, knocking over water bottles and scattering the contents of trash bags as they flailed.

BANG.

Ashleigh stumbled backward in reaction to the sound. The brief flash of light revealed the two men struggling over a gun—the gun Connor had dropped on the coffee table two days ago, the one they had used to rob the convenience store. The one that was supposedly unloaded.

The fighting men broke apart, and someone slumped to the floor.

Chapter 10

Every impulse in Ashleigh's body told her to run to the fallen man, but she clenched her leg muscles and resisted. Her ears ringing, she stepped quickly into the shadows in the corner of the room and turned her face away. She held her breath and listened intently for some indication of who held the gun. If it was Dean, all would be well. If it was Connor, her life would be in danger. She had kneed him in the groin, hit him with a flashlight, and rejected his apology. He had beaten people half to death for less.

"Ashleigh," Connor called, gasping for breath. "Ashleigh. Where are you, baby?" Cloth rustled and his footsteps moved across the floor. Ashleigh didn't breathe, every muscle in her body tense to the point of pain. She was starting to shake just when the community room door swung open and his footsteps moved into the hallway. The door swung shut behind him, and the next time he called for her, his voice was muffled.

Ashleigh let herself breathe and relaxed her body. When she was sure Connor had gone downstairs, she tiptoed across the room to Dean. He was curled up in a tight ball, and he seemed so small, like a roly poly, just a little harmless creature. She laid her hand on his bony shoulder. "Dean?"

He made no response. A dark shadow crept beneath him. Curious, Ashleigh leaned down impulsively and touched it. Her hand came away wet with warm, thick liquid. She whimpered.

She shook Dean's shoulder roughly. "Dean, c'mon. C'mon, man. Dean!"

His head flopped back and she saw, then, the damage Connor and his gun had done to Dean's face. She immediately looked away, her mind swimming with images of the exit wounds on the deer her father had hunted. The gun wasn't high-caliber, but at such close range it had made a dark cavern of Dean's nose. The moonlight limned the ragged edges of the wound in silver, the pointed bits of shattered bone, the gleam of blood that still pumped and oozed over the mangled flesh. His eyes were huge, white, and staring at nothing. His mouth hung open in an eternal question, blood pouring over his tongue and teeth, staining his t-shirt black.

It had been his favorite t-shirt, one he'd inherited from his older brother, who had purchased it at an actual Metallica concert. It was ruined, now.

Ashleigh jumped back from the corpse, crab-walking until she hit the wall. There she pressed herself against the cool concrete, breathed hard, and held back vomit, tears, screams, and the urge to run. None of these reactions would help her right now. They might, in fact, make her Connor's next victim. She forced the terror down, deep down, and let the cool, logical part of her brain take control. This was the part of her mind that had taken over when hunting with her father, when he forced her to skin dead animals and yank the entrails from the still-warm corpses. It could keep her moving and thinking while the panicked parts of her shrunk down so small they could fit neatly in one of those plastic bubbles from a toy dispenser.

She used the wall to push herself to her feet. Her foot bumped a bottle of water and, without thinking, she picked it up, unscrewed the cap, and took a swig. A plan began to form in her mind. She could hide in the asylum, sure, but there was a good chance Connor would find her eventually. She needed to hide somewhere secure, somewhere with a lock on the door. She would need supplies so she could outlast him, too, if he tried to wait her out.

With the flashlight in her waistband, Ashleigh gathered the bottles of water scattered around the room and stuffed them into a trash bag. Some were probably empty but she didn't have time to evaluate, only to act. She snatched up the backpack with the snack cakes and pulled it on her back. Then she used her free hands to grab one of the mattresses and pulled it toward the back of the community room.

The sound of footsteps on the stairs echoed up to her. A cat screamed, long and low, a warning sound.

"No no no no," Ashleigh whined, dragging the mattress into the bathroom. She swung the door shut and slammed the deadbolt into place.

A moment later, Connor pounded on the door with his fists. "Ashleigh! Come out of there."

Ashleigh dragged the mattress into the shower and pulled the shower curtain shut. She curled herself around the backpack and let herself sob.

Chapter 11

Connor pounded on the door and shouted for a long time, until his voice was hoarse and, she imagined, his hands must be bruised and aching. According to Ashleigh's phone, he stopped yelling and hitting the door close to eleven o'clock.

The phone still had no signal. Once Connor's heavy footfalls moved away from the door, Ashleigh crept to the small bathroom window, opened it, and stuck her hand out holding the phone, hoping for even a flicker of a bar. Nada.

She contemplated what to do next. Connor was undoubtedly going to try to find something he could use to attempt knocking the door down. Ashleigh didn't think there was much in the asylum that fit the bill, but she wasn't sure she wanted to take the chance. Her instinct was to run. Should she try to sneak away while he was searching? Where would she go? She had supplies and a mattress in here, plus plumbing. This was the best place in the asylum to survive a siege. With a resigned sigh, she decided to take her chances by staying in the bathroom.

She was exhausted, and slept for a time, a deep and dreamless sleep. When she roused, she pissed down one of the shower drains and then passed some time organizing the water bottles by how much water they contained. It was still nighttime, and even darker than before, as if the moon had gone into hiding, too. She fiddled with the flashlight, trying to get it to work, but she failed at that and eventually fell asleep again.

This time, she woke to the sound of something heavy and metal thudding against the bathroom door. "Aaaaash-leeeeeeeigh," Connor called. The sound of his voice made her skin want to crawl off her body and out the window.

Ashleigh crouched by the door with the flashlight at the ready. It was all she could do. Even as skinny as she was, she couldn't fit through the narrow window, and the drop to the concrete patio two floors down would probably break her ankles, anyway. She could only hope and pray Connor's arms gave out before the door did.

On the fourth strike, a dent appeared in the door. Ashleigh began to sob again. The flashlight shook in her hands. This was it. If Connor got through that door, she was as good as dead.

"Just open the door Ashleigh," Connor shouted, his words laced with menace. "I just want to talk."

THUD. An object poked through the dent, creating a crack.

"Just go away!" Ashleigh screamed, her voice high and hysterical. She didn't sound like herself.

"C'mon, baby. This isn't necessary. What happened to Dean was an accident. I didn't know the gun was loaded."

"GO AWAY!"

THUD. The crack in the door became a hole.

"Ash, just open the door. You're making me really angry—"

Connor's voice cut off, and then there was a heavy, metallic *BONG,* like the sound of a fire extinguisher hitting the floor. Silence followed, heavy as a down comforter.

Ashleigh dropped the flashlight to the floor with a clatter and covered her mouth with her hands. "Connor?"

No response was forthcoming. Had he suffered a heart attack? A stroke? That happened to meth users sometimes, out of nowhere, and he'd been using for a long time. She wondered if she should open the door and try to help him. But even if he was dying, what could she do? It's not as if she could call for an ambulance or drive him to the hospital.

Trembling so hard she could barely walk in a straight line, Ashleigh inched to the door and pressed her ear against it. She could hear something on the other side, but she wasn't sure what she was hearing: a grunt, a whimper, a gurgling sound. A new flavor of fear arced up her spine.

Could she just leave him there, suffering? Even if she couldn't help him, she could hold him while he died. Surely that was better than nothing.

But what if he was faking it to gain her sympathy and get her to open the door?

"Connor, are you okay?"

When there was still no answer, she reached up and slowly slid back the deadbolt. It was difficult now that the door was warped and required her to use both hands. She groped for the flashlight on the floor before she opened the door, slowly, cautiously, hoping she could yank it shut again if necessary.

The smell of hot iron smacked her in the face. She couldn't see much, just faint outlines, vague shapes in the darkness.

"Connor?"

The only answer was a soft shuffling sound. Ashleigh held her breath.

Something touched her leg and she jumped, screaming. She tried to scramble back into the bathroom but whatever it was stood between her and the door, forcing her to run out into the community room, where she slipped on something wet and went to the floor, hard, smacking her chin against the tile, the flashlight flying from her grip.

Groaning, Ashleigh pushed herself to her hands and knees and tried to get up. Pain lanced through her head and she had a sudden sense like she was falling, like the world was moving away from her, like everything was spinning and pulsing in a way that made it impossible to stand.

The clouds moved away from the moon and the room was suddenly bathed in silvery light again. Ashleigh wished the clouds hadn't moved. The light was not a blessing.

Less than a foot from her, a body lay sprawled on the floor. It was too big to be Dean or Kayla. The body's eyes stared at the ceiling and its jaw hung slack. She recognized the body's corded arms, splayed out as if he'd fallen backwards with his arms spread wide. Ashleigh didn't want to look at the rest of it, but the body jerked, and the hope that Connor was still alive flashed in her brain, and she lurched toward him on all fours.

"Connor," she rasped.

His throat was a yawning wound, a second dark mouth, lipless and wet. There were more slashes on his face and chest. The wounds were deep, long gashes with tidy edges, like they'd been made with a very sharp, very long knife.

Ashleigh was suddenly aware the killer must be in the room with her. Kayla was right. Someone lived in this asylum and wanted them dead, some crazy person. Images of a huge man wearing a mask made from someone else's face came unbidden to her mind's eye. He wore a filthy apron and wielded butcher knives.

More horror movie garbage, the logical part of her brain knew.

The logical part of her brain was outvoted by the rest of her, which was justifiably panicked. Ashleigh scrambled to her feet, slipping in—oh god, slipping in Connor's blood, it was everywhere, it was all over *her*—and she turned to run back into the bathroom, her den of safety, where she could hide from all this until morning, when sunlight would make it all better.

Something dark moved in front of the bathroom door, blocking her way, and she skidded to a halt, backing away from it, some primal fear activated. It was the size of a man, standing on two legs, and moonlight gleamed on its curved claws. Shadows shouldn't move, but here, in this asylum, in this place of madness, they did. Here, they stalked you, they hunted you, they blocked your way to refuge, and they smelled like ozone, wet fur, and blood.

A pair of green eyes opened and fixed their gaze on her, shockingly bright in the black-and-white movie of the moonlit community room.

Chapter 12

Ashleigh screamed, a sound of pure terror that ripped itself from her throat like she was regurgitating shards of glass. Her feet tried to carry her back, away from the eyes that hovered in the darkness, but she slipped on blood and went down on her ass, her tailbone striking the concrete so hard it forced a grunt from her mouth. The pain was blinding for an instant, and she sat gasping for a few seconds that felt like an eternity, all the world winnowed down to this one moment, this one point of agony. When her senses returned, she tried to rise, to flip over, to crawl, but with the pain that now radiated through her lower back and fear gripping her lungs, all she could do was flail and pull herself across the floor on her arms like a maimed mudskipper.

The door was far away, but the windows were closer. She pulled and pushed herself across the bloody floor, her breaths rasping, her heart pounding. Groaning, she grabbed the window frame and hauled herself up, up, up, inch by agonizing inch, until she was draped partway out the window.

Below her, the ground was concrete and too far away. She needed to go feet-first or she would likely break her neck, but maybe that was better than being slashed to death by some shadowy cat-thing.

A tug on her legs, and then she was hauled from the window frame. The creature had her by the ankle and dragged her away from the window. Closer to the source of light, she could see it a little better—and yet, it remained a shadow. It stood like a man, but its body wasn't a man's body, with joints facing the wrong directions. It was tall, over six feet, and the moonlight illuminated a coat of fine black fur across its body. And its face, its face was the most horrible part, those huge green eyes with massive black pupils staring out of a feline visage, with long fangs hanging over its bottom lip.

Even as she looked at it, though, the image seemed to waver, the edges of its body fraying and blending with the shadows, making it look larger and then smaller, giving the sensation that it was approaching her and melting back into the darkness simultaneously.

It made a sound, then, a sound like a grouchy cat scolding a kitten, a sound so like that menacing howl she had heard on her first night at the asylum.

Adrenaline making her forget her broken tailbone, Ashleigh lashed out with her free foot and kicked as hard as she could. The creature released her with a hiss, and she threw her feet out the window and followed them without thinking. She didn't decide to fling herself out of a second-story window, she just did it.

The concrete patio met her faster than she expected. One of her ankles snapped. She hit the ground hard, but somehow managed to protect her head. New pain searing through her, the breath knocked from her body, Ashleigh lay staring up at the moon for a few moments, her vision ragged and narrowing rapidly. She fought against the urge to lose consciousness, checking in with her body part by part: hands, legs, head, chest. She could feel them all, and operate them all, though when she tried to move her right leg, searing pain started in her ankle and burned all the way up her leg to join with the terrible ache in her ass, her lower back, her chest.

Her body was broken. She wanted to give up. It would be so much easier than trying to live, and she'd been trying to die for so long. But the images of Dean's ruined face and Connor's ravaged throat came to her mind, and she forced herself to stand, bit by aching bit, until she was mostly upright.

She couldn't put much weight on her right foot, so limping to the trees took much too long. She leaned on a sapling and looked back at the asylum. Nothing moved in the moonlight except trees swaying in the breeze. Had the thing not followed her? Maybe it was trapped in the asylum and couldn't leave. That wouldn't explain the grotesquely murdered coyote they had found, but maybe that was created by something else.

Ashleigh picked up a long stick and used it like a cane to shuffle forward. The forest was thick with darkness, the canopy blocking out the moon's gift of light, making the ground a mystery. She moved carefully rather than quickly, weeping, crying out loudly each time she moved her tailbone or her ankle too much and fresh pain blossomed inside her like a burning ember. She wished for Connor, who would have been able to carry her away from here in his big, strong arms. She wished for her father. She wished for Dean and even Kayla, and that's when she realized: Kayla had run away.

Kayla might still be alive.

"Kayla," she whimpered, and then she screamed it. She limped forward, shouting her friend's name through her sobs, a ragged, desperate sound.

A sunken spot in the forest floor made her lose her balance and she fell forward, issuing a cry of frustration and disappointment as she hit the leaf-strewn ground. Branches scratched mercilessly at her face and arms as she fell. Gasping, clutching at the dirt, she tried to force herself up, but she couldn't. Her left ankle was stuck in the hole she had stepped in, and she cursed whatever animal had dug it.

The only thing she could do was tip her head back and use her last conscious breath to scream, a wordless, horrified sound that echoed through the forest.

Chapter 13

Ashleigh regained consciousness lying on her back on something soft. She opened her eyes expecting to see a nurse hovering over her in a spare white-walled hospital room. She prepared to apologize to Kayla and embrace her for saving her life.

Instead, she let out a long, low groan, making a single word: "No."

She was back in the asylum.

Sunlight streamed in through the filthy windows, illuminating one of the dorm rooms. She was lying on a cot, with a patchy blanket draped over her and a mildew-smelling pillow behind her head.

Her tailbone throbbed and her ankle pulsed. Pain and hunger made her stomach clench tight as a fist.

Ashleigh tore the blanket from her body and tried to sit up but hesitated, staring at her ankle.

Her shoes had been removed and placed carefully beside the bed. Her ankle had been bandaged with what looked like clean, white bandages, and the skin around the bandages was pinker, cleared of dirt and blood.

It still hurt, it was still broken, but someone had cleaned and bandaged her broken ankle.

She didn't remember being carried back to the asylum. She didn't remember anything that had happened after her unwise trek into the forest. Where had she been trying to go? Just...away. Away from this terrible place. Away from...

Her clothes were stained with blood, more brown than red. Connor's blood. Dean's blood. The memories of what had occurred the night before were like a spike to her brain. She fought down the urge to cry and called up the logical part of her mind, the cold and rational part. The only person who could have saved her was Kayla. She wasn't a big woman, but she was taller than Ashleigh so maybe she had found a way to bring her back to the asylum.

Hesitantly, she called, "Kayla?"

When there was no answer except the distant yowling of cats somewhere beyond the door of her room, she considered other options. Kayla was the most logical choice, but maybe she wasn't the only one on the mountain. Maybe someone else was here. Maybe Kayla's serial killer wasn't a serial killer at all, but someone like them, someone just looking to hide away from the world.

Then why hadn't they revealed themself before now?

Maybe her dad had tracked her phone to this place and come to rescue her. That seemed more likely. But then where was he? And why did he bring her back to the asylum rather than carrying her down the mountain to safety? None of this made sense.

Ashleigh was thirsty, hungry, and needed to pee. She slid from the bed and swallowed against the pain that threatened to send her into the darkness again when she placed weight on her left foot. She didn't want to go into the hallway barefoot, but she didn't think she could manage her shoes. With a sigh of resignation, she hopped to the door and out into the corridor, which still smelled powerfully of ammonia. There was a bathroom across the hall, and she used the toilet though it contained no water and wouldn't flush. Using a proper toilet felt like a small luxury she could grant herself now that her situation was so dire.

Afterward, she stood in the dim hallway, staring at the community room's doors with their stained glass. Her water and food was in there. She needed both, but there was no way she was going back in there, not after what happened last night. She could almost taste the metallic tang of blood on her tongue. Dean's hollow face and Connor's slashed throat appeared before her like a mirage.

Ashleigh went back to bed and hoped her mysterious nurse would bring her what she needed to survive. She had struggled so hard to live the night before, but now she felt resigned to die in this awful, cursed place. Eventually, she slept.

When she woke again it was dusk, the room drenched in gray. The door was open, and a silhouette filled it.

Ashleigh sat up. "Kayla?" The silhouette swayed but didn't enter the room. It was too tall and muscular to be Kayla. "D-dad?" The word came out choked, like she was being gently strangled.

She knew it wasn't Kayla, or her dad.

It was the shadow-man with the cat face.

He glided into the room, filling it with the scent of the forest, piney and loamy. His luminous green eyes fixed on her face. In the twilight, he was more solid—now she could see the long tail lashing behind him, curling and uncurling as if reflecting his curiosity—but everywhere shadow touched him, he joined with it, bleeding into it, becoming one with it. What had frightened her the night before—the fangs, the fur, the slope of his snout, the movement of his limbs—was suddenly elegant, beautiful, like something an artist would create in a fever-dream.

The shadow-man moved to sit on the bed beside her like ink flowing from a pen, all liquid grace. His claws were gone, and the hand (or paw?) he placed over hers on the bed was warm and soft.

A sound emanated from him, like a whirring motor. Was he *purring*? Ashleigh licked her lips. "Did you bring me back here?"

He did not respond. Instead, he turned to examine her ankle, lifting it gently, inspecting the bandages, and then lowering it again.

"I need water, and food," she said, gesturing with her hand to her mouth.

The shadow-man rose abruptly, stalking out of the room so quickly it felt instantaneous. He returned moments later, padding on silent feet, with a bottle of water and the bag of snack cakes.

Ashleigh guzzled half the water and fell on the snack cakes like a ravenous wolf. The shadow-man watched her and purred while she ate. She wanted to pretend he wasn't there, but as night threw a black veil over the room it became impossible to ignore the twin lanterns of his eyes.

When she was done, she sank back down onto the bed, suddenly exhausted, pulling the blanket up to her chin. The shadow-man watched her movements with his intense gaze.

From this angle, she could see past him, to the door of the room. A handful of cats had gathered there. They watched him, and her, and blinked their shining eyes slowly, tails flicking across the floor.

He leaned forward, his face so close she could feel his breath. His fangs seemed even bigger up close. She couldn't help imagining them tearing into her throat. She squeezed her eyes shut.

Something soft bumped her chin and rubbed its way up her cheek. She gasped with the realization that he was mashing his face into her neck and jaw. She opened her eyes to see that his were closed, and somehow she knew, though she knew little of cats, that this was a marker of affection.

The next thing she knew, his purring body had climbed into the bed with her and his long, dark arms were wrapped around her body. He smelled like decaying leaves and smoke.

Ashleigh tensed so hard she thought she might snap in two. A few tears dripped down the sides of her face.

The shadow-man regarded her from mere inches away with those huge, round eyes, his pupils so massive only a thin ring of green remained around the edges. The purring never stopped—in fact, it intensified until it seemed to vibrate the bed and her body. Unexpectedly, he leaned close to her and licked the side of her face, lapping up her tears. His whiskers tickled her cheek.

Ashleigh relaxed. He wasn't going to harm her. He had saved her life—twice, if you counted murdering Connor, though she preferred not to think about that. It would be ridiculous for him to go to all the trouble of rescuing her and bandaging her wounds only to kill her.

Now that she had relaxed, the purr seemed to penetrate her skin, her muscles, her bones. It vibrated every cell of her body. The pain in her tailbone and ankle was forgotten, drowned out by the hum of the shadow-man.

Ashleigh sank into his arms, letting herself enjoy the velvet of his fur, the strength of his embrace. Who would have thought, she marveled, that shadows would be so luxuriously soft? Several cats jumped up onto the bed and made themselves comfortable, and Ashleigh reached out and scratched the ears of the nearest one. The shadow-man seemed to approve, nestling his face into the crook of her shoulder.

With a sigh of contentment, Ashleigh let herself drift back into sleep.

Chapter 14

Ashleigh spent a few days and nights in the shadow-man's care. He brought her food and water, checked her bandages, and wrapped himself around her with his warm body, his purr sinking into her soul. When the shakes hit, and the nausea, and she wanted meth so much she would have murdered her own child for it, he held her and purred while she screamed and cried, until the burning need had passed and she came out of it a person again.

By the end of a week—she wasn't sure how long it had really been, because time was fluid without clear boundaries—she was able to stand on her broken ankle, making her think perhaps it hadn't been broken at all. Her tailbone bruise seemed like a distant memory. She managed to hobble down the stairs, and at dusk the shadow-man found her on the patio playing with some kittens with a water bottle lid.

He dove for her, rubbing his face against her body, his long tail looping around her waist and stroking up her chest. If she didn't know better, she'd think the creature was trying to seduce her. She laughed and slapped his tail away. He crouched on the ground beside her, blinking those magnificent eyes up at her. She blinked back at him, slowly, and this seemed to please him, because he started purring immediately.

"Friend," Ashleigh whispered. (She refused to call him Perry.) "I'm feeling much better. It might be time for me to go home."

The shadow-man's head twisted this way and that, as if he were trying to comprehend her words, but she knew he wouldn't understand. He never did. They communicated mainly through touch and pantomime. This concept was more abstract than anything she had tried to communicate to him before, though, and she frowned. Finally, she gestured down the mountain. "Home. I want to go back to Perrysville."

He reared back and hissed.

Ashleigh dropped her arm and froze. He'd never been angry or upset with her before. Her mind flashed to the mangled coyote, to Connor's bloody face. Though he put them away when he was with her, the shadow-man possessed claws like a bear's and fangs like a tiger's. She had forgotten that, in her complacency, but now she remembered in a flash of panic.

She lowered her eyes and held back tears. She couldn't hobble down the mountain on her own, not yet, but when she could, would he let her leave? His reaction made it seem like he wouldn't. Would she be trapped here forever? The idea had its merits—no one had ever cared for her so lovingly as the shadow-man—but, unexpectedly, she missed her dad and stepmom. She missed conversation, and showers, and watching TV. She longed for a cold, fizzy Coke, a hamburger with cheese, and a bag of Skittles. She would have given her left leg for a Styrofoam container full of fried rice from the Chinese place on Gilson Avenue.

Fried rice was Connor's favorite food. Her heart clenched tight and she pressed her hand to her sternum. They'd eaten it every Friday night, everyone clustered around two Styrofoam containers, when Kayla would pick some up on the way home from work.

Kayla. Ashleigh's only hope, now, was the woman she had thrown to the floor and hit in the head with a flashlight. If Kayla had made it down the mountain, maybe she would tell someone about the squatters at the asylum. Maybe the police would come. Jail might be an improvement over this—at least it wouldn't smell like cat piss and she'd get to bathe once in a while.

A long, soft tail rubbed against her arm and encircled her waist. The shadow-man pulled her to him, ever so gently. His arms embraced her and the sound of his purrs drowned out the rest of the world, the delightful vibration pushing out other thoughts. She could feel the tips of his claws against her skin where his hands rested on her back. She understood, then, on a visceral level, that even though he could, he would never harm her.

As long as she stayed.

In one smooth motion, he lifted her the way Connor had done only days before. She didn't bring her legs up to encircle his waist but clung to him all the same. She had grown accustomed to his smell like the earth just before the rain and the feel of his silken fur under her fingers.

He carried her into the asylum and to her room, placing her on the bed. The rusty springs of the ancient mattress shrieked beneath her. He undressed her slowly, wonderingly, running satin fingers across her skin with each newly revealed part of her body. His every touch was gentle and reverent, and his care for her pleasure was thorough. They didn't speak the same language at all, but it didn't matter; it was as if he knew the language of her body and could interpret every whimper and moan, every gasp, shiver, and muscle clench, playing her as deftly as a musician plays an instrument. Sometimes she caught herself just watching him, struck by the beauty of his strange form, the way the edges of his body melded into the shadows and then curled magically into muscles and fur, the way his eyelids fluttered, his eyes becoming brilliant green jewels as her pleasure mounted to a climax.

She thought of Connor when the shadow-man nipped her breasts, when he knelt between her legs and lapped at her wetness, and when he nuzzled her neck with his hot breath. As fireworks exploded inside her, so did shame, unfurling like the black sails on a ship that would carry her to oblivion. She missed Connor with a ferocity that forced tears from her eyes.

Ashleigh sobbed as the shadow-man climbed on top of her, licking away her tears, pushing himself inside her. He was soft and warm and the pressure of him was comforting, the weight of his shadowy form covering her, the familiar hardness between her legs making her clench down and groan with longing. His fangs were sharp on her nipples, his hands and tail touching her everywhere, seeking every inch of flesh, as if he would devour her.

Another orgasm tore through her, making her flail and gasp as pleasure seemed to infiltrate every cell in her body. It was maybe the most intense orgasm she'd ever had. After, she trembled as he continued moving inside her, ashamed of herself for finding pleasure with a creature who didn't even have a human face. She felt like she was betraying Connor, who lay dead at the end of the hall, murdered by the very creature that now arched his back and howled, burying himself between her legs.

The shadow-man shattered around her, the orgasm literally taking him apart. Ashleigh was enveloped in velvety darkness that blotted out the moonlight, the dorm room, reality itself. She should have been frightened, but instead she felt free. In the darkness there was no fear, no hunger, no itching or aching. She felt like she was floating, bodiless, in a magnificent obsidian pool. She could have stayed there forever.

He began to coalesce again, the edges of his body bleeding into the shadows so the only anchor to corporeality seemed to be his eyes, which glowed like neon, brighter than she had ever seen them before. And then his form dispersed suddenly into the many shadows in the dark room. Ashleigh grasped at the air, but he slipped through her fingers like smoke. The smell of him lingered in the room for a few moments and then was gone.

Ashleigh called for him and cried, trembling, suddenly cold and alone.

Chapter 15

A few cats pushed their way into the room and jumped up on the bed to lay on and around her, their warm bodies and soft purrs a poor replacement for the shadow-man's loving arms and bone-vibrating purrs. She lay awake, wishing for his embrace, suddenly frightened by the sounds outside her window.

A weird combination of emotions made a tight ball in her stomach. She did not want to stay in the asylum, but the shadow-man was so good to her. How could she leave him? Even if he had killed Connor—he'd done it to save her, after all. She should stay out of gratitude. She should forgo all the pleasures and conveniences of human civilization to remain with the shadow-man and be his paramour. It's what she deserved. Hadn't she brought everyone here? In the end, wasn't she responsible for their deaths?

Maybe this was purgatory, where she had to endure the torture of having to choose between a life with the shadow-man here in this nightmare place, or a life without him back in the comfort of the human world. Neither one appealed to her completely.

But she realized, with a cold sensation of crystallization in her belly, she was done being love's bitch. She thought of Connor and

Kayla and the wet slap of flesh, the smell of sex, and Kayla's soft, desperate cries. Whatever else happened, Ashleigh wouldn't put a man ahead of her own needs ever again. As kind and loving as the shadow-man was, he couldn't give her the things she wanted: a home, maybe a baby, or even a conversation. To stay here would be surrendering to another Connor. He would have what he wanted, and she would be the obedient slave to his attention.

In the morning, she dressed and ate the snack cakes the shadow-man had left for her. She wasn't sure where he was getting the food, but he seemed to be convinced she ate only junk, and she was so tired of Twinkies she could barf. Still, she forced herself to choke them down so she would have the energy to do what she needed to do. She gulped down some water from the fresh bottle he had brought her and then put the water bottle in her pocket.

Her dead cell phone carefully placed in her other pocket, she exited the asylum under the watchful eyes of its feline denizens and knew her actions would be reported back to their master in the evening. Thinking of Connor, she found a huge stick and used it to clear the path before her as she marched down the grassy road. Insects and other small creatures jumped and scurried from her path. The forest made chirping and croaking sounds on either side of the grass as if to warn her from entering the tree line.

The walk was not unpleasant. With her phone dead, Ashleigh could only estimate how long it took, but with her heart full of hope, it didn't seem like torture. In fact, it was nice to stretch her legs, nice to feel the sun on her limbs, even if the weather was cooler than was appropriate for her tiny shorts. She wished she had the scratchy sweater, but she'd burned it, unwilling to wear it again because of the blood stains.

She saw the car peeking out over the grass and walked faster, excitement making blood rush in her ears. She hit something with her stick but didn't stop in time and tripped over it, sending her sprawling into the grass, her chin bouncing painfully against the dirt. Groaning, she struggled to her feet and used the stick to part the long blades of grass, investigating what had so rudely tripped her. She expected a log, a tree trunk, maybe a large rock.

It was a human leg. The skin was mottled purple and red, but even so, Ashleigh thought it looked familiar. She pushed the grass aside: the leg was wearing a sneaker. A sneaker she knew: Kayla's sneaker.

Ashleigh groaned. She dropped the stick and used her hands to part the grass so she could see the rest of the body. Kayla's face was sunken and her skin gray, but her yellow ponytail was still intact. A stench came up off the rotten flesh and Ashleigh turned away. What had happened to her friend? There were no signs of slash wounds, so the shadow-man hadn't gotten her the way he'd gotten Connor. Ashleigh didn't see any evidence of gunshot wounds, either. She parted the grass over the purple leg and saw them, then: holes, multiple holes in Kayla's leg like someone had taken sewing needles to her skin, again and again.

Panicking, Ashleigh swept at the grass with her stick looking for any sign of rattlesnakes. Kayla must have disturbed an entire nest to have so many bites. Timber rattler venom could be survived, but not when the victim had been bitten so many times, not without help from a hospital. Ashleigh tried not to think about how painful, miserable, and lonely Kayla's death must have been, but tears rose to her eyes anyway. She had told Kayla to leave in the middle of the night. She had hit her, and shamed her, and called her names. Kayla might still be alive if Ashleigh hadn't been so angry, so cruel, and so volatile.

Ashleigh cleared a wide path to the car, even sliding the stick under the vehicle to make sure nothing lurked there. The tires were flat, just as Kayla had said. Ashleigh grabbed the door handle to find it locked.

Locked.

She turned slowly and looked back at Kayla's exposed leg. She'd been hoping the keys would be in the car, because why would Kayla take them back to the asylum with her? It's not as if anyone was going to steal a car with slashed tires. It's not as if there was anyone up here to even steal the car.

But Kayla had locked the doors and kept the keys with her.

Ashleigh swallowed hard. She didn't want to look at Kayla's body, didn't want to smell it, and most definitely didn't want to touch it. But she was going to have to do all three to get the car keys.

She told herself to do it quickly, to get it over with, but her legs wouldn't obey. She approached the corpse slowly, cautiously, as if it would get up and take a bite out of her. She tried to forget all the zombie movies she'd watched as a kid, tried not to remember the chomp of their teeth into fresh, living flesh.

Shame crawled over her when she made it to Kayla's torso. Her flesh was desiccated, withered to the bone and rotting away. Her friend wasn't going to get back up, no matter how much Ashleigh might secretly want her to lunge forward and take a pound of flesh in retribution for Ashleigh's role in her death.

Kayla lay there, stinking, and Ashleigh reached carefully into her pocket and removed the keys, and that was it.

Ashleigh pressed the button to unlock the doors and climbed into the passenger seat. The car was oppressively hot. She climbed over the center console and into the driver's seat, put the key in the ignition, and started the car. It sputtered to life and she issued a gust of relieved laughter. With trembling hands, she found the charging cable and plugged in her phone.

Then, she waited with the windows down while her phone charged. She had no choice but to rest.

Bright eyes watched her from the tree line, the shadow-man's spies.

When her phone was charged, she turned it on and couldn't help issuing a happy laugh. The time was 10:42 AM. She had no signal. She had already tried walking up the mountain to get a better signal, and it hadn't worked, so this time, she trudged down the hillside, sweeping at the grass with her stick. At least now she could walk on overgrown gravel and, eventually, on asphalt. She walked quickly, at first, eager to get away from Kayla's reeking corpse, but soon she had to slow, unable to keep up the pace on an ankle that, while healed, was still wobbly.

This walk was unbearably long compared to the walk to the car. Ashleigh's exertions had made her hungry and her stomach growled. She finished the last of the water in the bottle and tossed it into the trees. Littering felt like a final "fuck you" to the mountainside that had taken her friends.

At first, she checked for bars every few steps, but eventually it became clear that was a futile effort. She counted to fifty before checking. Then one hundred.

It was nearly two o'clock in the afternoon before she was too exhausted to continue without a rest. She sank to the asphalt without ceremony, leaning on the stick that had become a walking stick now that sweeping the grass for snakes was no longer necessary.

Cats melted out of the shadows on the mountainside, watching her. She wondered how far they would follow. Would they tell the shadow-man where she lived? The thought made her gut churn. He might be angry she had left him. He might try to carry her back up the mountainside. Returning to the asylum was out of the question. Ashleigh would die first.

She pulled out her phone to check the time and gasped. She had two bars. Two tiny bars of hope. She mashed the auto-dial for her dad's number and cleared her throat even as a stone became lodged in her trachea and tears started pouring down her cheeks. The phone rang only twice.

"Ashleigh? Is that you?"

Chapter 16

The quiet of the hospital bothered Ashleigh, at first. Her parents were pleased she had a private room, but she wished for a roommate. There were no kittens meowing high-pitched pleas for milk, no tomcats screaming for dominance, no birds warbling and wailing, no friends bustling about. The hospital felt dead compared to the asylum.

She struggled to sleep the first few nights, convinced the shadow-man would come for her. She stared wide-eyed out the huge window and babbled about how the hospital security didn't matter, because the shadow-man was made of literal shadow and could slip through the crack under the door, until they sedated her. Then she slept like the dead.

Weirdly enough, though she feared he would drag her back to the asylum, Ashleigh missed her inhuman lover, especially when she was lonely and cold, and her body ached. She remembered his strong arms, his soft fur, and the powerful hum of his purr and it was as if her bones longed for him. Some days, she wept in fear and others, she wept with longing. Other days, she lay despondent, despair draped over her like a mourning shroud.

The police came and interviewed her after a few weeks. By then she was sensible enough not to mention that Connor's murderer and her rescuer was a cat-man made of shadows. Instead, when they asked her to describe what the knife-wielding maniac had looked like, she shrugged and said it had been too dark to see his face. The detectives seemed unsatisfied with this answer but they left anyway, saying they would be in touch if they had any more questions.

Ashleigh doubted they would. Connor wasn't exactly a model citizen. As long as his killer didn't leave the mountain and kill anybody else, nobody would care.

Her first few days at the hospital she could barely eat. Everything had the texture of a sponge and tasted like sugar and artificial flavoring. Within a week, however, she became incredibly hungry, eating everything the hospital offered her and whatever her parents brought, even foods she didn't like. The doctors said that was a good sign. Ashleigh stood in front of the bathroom mirror and pulled the cotton hospital gown taut against her slim body so she could see the new curve of her belly. Everyone thought she was just gaining much-needed weight. They were so excited.

But Ashleigh knew different. She placed her hand over her abdomen, feeling something flutter beneath her skin, imagining shadows roiling and thrashing within her.

To put her mind at ease, the doctors tested her for pregnancy three times before they wouldn't test her anymore. All three tests came back negative. Ashleigh sobbed hysterically until they sedated her again.

She knew she was either losing her mind or bearing an impossible child; both options were equally unappealing.

On the day she was scheduled to be discharged, her dad told her the asylum was going to be torn down. The demolition was scheduled, and the only challenge was getting the equipment up the steep mountainside without proper roads. "But they'll manage," he assured her, squeezing her hand as if he was afraid the news would send her spiraling into another episode of inarticulate screaming.

Ashleigh only nodded. "Probably for the best," she whispered. Her mind flashed to Connor's throat gleaming wetly in the moonlight, Dean's face transformed into a bowl of blood, and Kayla's desiccated corpse in the grass. She swallowed the painful lump that rose in her throat.

"Ready to go?" Dad asked, gesturing to the wheelchair the hospital had provided.

Ashleigh pressed a hand to her swollen abdomen and chewed her lower lip. The shadows under her skin were still and silent, for now, in the daylight. She missed Connor with a clench in her stomach, like a fist was closing around it. A familiar smoky, acrid flavor filled her mouth and her nose. Her veins pulsed with need. She swayed in place, ragged with craving.

Her dad pressed her gently into the wheelchair. "It'll be okay," he murmured, squeezing her shoulder.

Ashleigh didn't respond. If there was one thing she knew, it was that things were not going to be okay. Not ever again.

Dad pushed the wheelchair down the hall, into the elevator, and out the hospital doors, into the sunlight. Ashleigh stood in the light, squinting against the brightness, her hand raised, waiting for him to bring the car around. Her eyes were drawn upward, to the mountainside, where the asylum still squatted, a harsh man-made line against the pulpy gray sky.

Like it was waiting for her. Beckoning her. And she knew, even if they tore it down, even once nature had reclaimed the land where it once stood, the asylum would still call to her with an insistent pressure in the front of her brain. It would haunt her dreams with the reek of blood and ammonia. Shadows would always undulate out of the corner of her eye.

With Connor gone, she wasn't sure where to get what she needed to blot out the asylum's influence, but she would figure it out. She always did.

Afterword

One bad decision leads to another, which opens up a world that neither Ashleigh, nor the reader, ever saw coming in Sarah Hans' *Asylum*, the next entry in the *Selected Papers from the Consortium for the Study of Anomalous Phenomena*. Hans treats readers to a journey as they watch Ashleigh traverse a tightwire of emotions and treacherous situations only to find herself in an unfathomable reality. You see, she is with child, or so she thinks, but what she is carrying no one has ever seen the likes of... and the craving that plagues her hasn't abated.

Drugs, abuse, betrayal, and a tryst under the moonlight with an otherworldly being round out Ashleigh's trip to the woods, a place she ended up because she was running from a series of bad decisions that both she and her boyfriend made. It is this whirlwind of causes and responses that will leave the reader breathless and mired in the muck of a place they can't identify... one they are too afraid to explore.

Hans deftly carries readers along on this trip of their nightmares, telling them it's ok to be afraid, to sidestep the blood that stands in their way, and to enjoy the music of the cats that serenade them. To do anything more would be to look the beast directly in the eyes and, well, we all know that no good ever comes from that.

Spine-tingling fun!

L. Marie Wood
Author of *12 Hours*

About the Author

Sarah Hans is an award-winning writer, editor, and teacher whose stories have appeared in more than 40 publications, including *Apex Magazine* and *Pseudopod*. She's also the author of several books, including the horror novel *Entomophobia* and the children's picture book *Goodnight Halloween*. You can find her on Twitter, Instagram, and TikTok under the handle @witchwithabook, where she loves to talk about what she's reading. She lives in Ohio with her partner, the best stepkids in the galaxy, and a small circus of pets.

www.ingramcontent.com/pod-product-compliance
Lightning Source LLC
Chambersburg PA
CBHW050905180626
46814CB00007B/2904